"You're holding

Judy said, staring at   t this
far without hopping

"But you, my sin   f the
credit," Sonya laughed.

"Oh, but that husband of yours helped you through the
hardest stretch when he chimed in."

Sonya sat on the corner of the bed. "You know, you're
right. I can hardly remember the last part of the ride. I don't
want to remember!"

"You two seem close. You care about each other deeply,
even when you have your differences."

Sonya stiffened. *Close?* "We haven't been close for a long
time, believe it or not. I was hoping this trip would have that
effect, though."

"Well, it looks like your plan is working."

KAREN HAYSE is an enthusiastic fifth grade teacher. Her husband, Mark, teaches too, as professor of religion at MidAmerica Nazarene College. They have a teenage daugher, Melinda. The couple have spent some of their most memorable vacations biking on the Missouri Katy Trail. When Karen is not teaching, writing, or biking, she loves to stay active playing tennis and co-ed volleyball. She also covets stillness, and teaches an all-women Sunday school class. Karen has co-written a book for mothers, *Through the Generations*, with her own mother, Charlotte Adelsperger.

The Flat Marriage Fix

Karen Hayse

Heartsong Presents

To my mom, writer Charlotte Adelsperger, who encouraged the Katy Trail setting, and to my biking buddy and husband of sixteen sweet years, Mark Hayse.

A note from the Author:
I love to hear from my readers! You may correspond with me by writing:

Karen Hayse
Author Relations
PO Box 719
Uhrichsville, OH 44683

ISBN 1-59310-491-X

THE FLAT MARRIAGE FIX

Our mission is to publish and distribute inspirational products offering exceptional value and biblical encouragement to the masses.

All scripture quotations, unless otherwise indicated, are taken from the HOLY BIBLE, NEW INTERNATIONAL VERSION®. NIV®. Copyright © 1973, 1978, 1984 by International Bible Society. Used by permission of Zondervan. All rights reserved.

All of the characters and events in this book are fictitious. Any resemblance to actual persons, living or dead, or to actual events is purely coincidental.

PRINTED IN THE U.S.A.

Or check out our Web site at www.heartsongpresents.com

prologue

It wasn't Christmas. Not her birthday either. It was September, when gifts were an afterthought. And yet, Sonya Kane felt that magical holiday anticipation the minute her husband, Brad, escorted her to the second floor of Cardwell's Department Store. She *knew* what they sold on the second floor.

And when they stopped where her suspicions predicted, she had to hold back the tears. Theoretically, these unexpected gifts weren't even for *her*, and that made them even more touching.

She was surprised, yet she wasn't. Brad, her husband of two years and three months had found another way to say that she was the sun that belonged in his tranquil sky.

"I thought I was coming along to help you pick out a dress shirt," Sonya said, looking in their cart, which held nothing whatsoever from the men's department. "I still can't believe you brought me here for this. You hate to shop, Brad. You simply hate it!"

Brad shrugged and looked away. He never flaunted or wore his pride out in the open. That was not his way. Brad Kane was unassuming, never melodramatic. Able to say a great deal without saying much.

Her polar opposite.

And yet, there they were, the two of them flipping through doll-sized hangers on a circular rack. Brad sized up miniature dresses against Sonya's widening waist and said things like, "Hmm. . .I don't think it will fit. But it sure is cute." And he'd toss the ruffled outfits in the basket. He hated shopping with a passion, but today showed that he loved her with even more intensity than that.

Giggling, the couple made their way through the maze of

steel racks, stopping at the sales counter. After the cashier scanned the final dress, she quoted the grand total.

Brad clicked his ballpoint and filled in the lines of his check. With a tidy rip, he offered it to the navy-suited woman. "Here." He clicked the pen, shot a boyish grin, and got a healthy grip on the crinkled paper sack. "And here," he said, this time to Sonya, handing her the bag. "For Maggie, the best dressed baby in the state of Illinois."

"She's not even born yet."

"As soon as she is. . ."

Sonya took the sack, not able to stop herself from peeking in for another look. Ribbons and lace and nursery rhyme flannel were stacked in neat folds. In two months. . .oh, she could hardly wait! Now Brad, her man of few words, had *shown* that he felt the same way. *He* had dragged Sonya to the tiny garments—not the other way around as she had imagined it would happen.

Brad slid his fingers in her empty hand. With an affectionate wink, they were off.

They walked (Sonya on the verge of waddling) tile by gleaming tile, past the ceiling-high curtain displays, next to the coffee tables, right by the—

"I need to sit down." She plopped down in an azure recliner before Brad had a chance to object. "I'm sorry. You know. . .my feet, my back. They're not the same."

"Don't apologize." Brad leaned down and pulled the lever on her footrest.

Every muscle and bone in Sonya's haggard body settled to a neutral state of bliss. Her eyelids dropped, transporting her away from the vast department store. She sighed. "We *have* to get one of these." She felt a kiss brush her cheek, then her automatic smile. "Give me one more minute, Brad. Then I'll be ready to move on. At least to the bed displays. But don't let me stop there. If I do, I might never—"

"Rest as long as you want, hon."

A nasal voice joined in. "That's one of our best sellers."

Sonya opened her eyes to yet another navy-suited sales representative. Her tag read Marguerite. Sonya lifted her head.

"My wife—she's expecting," Brad interjected. "It's okay if she rests here for a minute, isn't it?"

"Of course." Marguerite pulled a card from her pressed coat and waved it toward the register. "I'm over there if you need me."

Brad took the card and buried it in his jeans pocket. He lowered his weight to a floral recliner next to Sonya, perching on its edge.

"I'm getting up," she said. But she couldn't manage so much as a twitch. Her mind traveled to their saggy, secondhand living room set. "Actually, I really do want it."

"What? The chair?" Brad leaned to flip the plastic sleeve that held the price tag. "Oh. . .Sonya. I'd love to, but—"

"I need this chair. I'm gaining weight by the hour."

He kneeled down next to her. "You may be tired, you may be hormonal, but you're not gaining weight. Weight is what I lift at the health club. It's what women try to get rid of. This"—he patted her tummy—"is a beauty mark."

His eyes twinkled with conviction. Every so often, he would ramble like that. And usually, she wished he would not stop. This was no exception. Still, the chair—

"Change your mind yet?" The sales rep returned.

Brad's jaw fell open only halfway before a "Yes!" escaped Sonya's mouth. She watched Brad's hand go to his pocket and push his billfold deeper inside.

Marguerite rattled off a prepackaged speech as Sonya showed Brad her best pleading eyes.

"It's a little steep," Brad said. "Anything a little, um—for lack of words—*cheaper*?"

The woman pointed to some flimsy models that looked as if they might not survive the delivery drive home.

Sonya leaned toward her husband. "I was hoping you'd understand that I will need something more substantial than those boxy chairs we have at home. After Maggie comes, you can lounge around in this silly chair as much as you want. I promise. So at least *try* it."

He slowly dropped the footrest and offered Sonya a hand. With a heave and a pull, the two traded places. Sonya tried not to smile when the wrinkles in Brad's forehead melted away. She said, "What did I tell you? Nice, huh?"

"Listen." Marguerite's foghorn voice tried unsuccessfully to whisper. "We *do* have the same chair at a discount in back. It has a small rip on the side, and it would be more cost effective for us to sell it at a discount than to reupholster." She quoted a staggeringly low figure. "Want to look?"

Sonya nodded furiously, and Brad didn't object. The couple followed the sales rep through an employee door.

"Here it is!" Marguerite motioned to an overstuffed lounger at her right.

"It doesn't look the same," Brad said. "My wife wanted the Bartlett model."

"It *is* the Bartlett. In mocha."

Brad turned to Sonya. "Do you want a *brown* chair, honey?"

It was a bit drab. But she would be sitting in it, not wearing it. "I don't care. I'd take construction cone orange if it was all they had in stock. Especially at that price."

"That settles it," Brad said, offering Marguerite a handshake. His eyes crinkled in a smile. "Wrap up one mocha recliner for the beautiful young lady."

Christmas or not, Sonya didn't need mistletoe to show him how she felt.

one

Six years later

Brad Kane steered home. Not fast; nothing prompted him. Not slow; he wasn't dreading his arrival either. Just medium speed. Run of the mill. Average. Just as he was sure another night at home would be. Once there, he lugged his duffel bag to the front porch, unlocked the door, and marched through the living room to the study, straight to his favorite spot—the brown Bartlett recliner.

"Hello? Brad?" The voice came from the kitchen.

He hesitated to answer. He had just spent all day with clients at the health club where he worked. What he needed was unadulterated quiet. Unfortunately, Sonya's middle name was Chatterbox. "Hi, Sonya," he finally said. Not loudly, for he already heard the rapid staccato of her steps growing louder.

"Honey, here's some iced tea," she said, beside him now. "It's that kind you like—you know, bottled green tea with a splash of ginger peach. That *is* it, right?"

"Sure." Green, peach, plain, whatever. He took it and smiled tightly.

Sonya sat on the arm of the chair and crossed her thick legs. "I've started guzzling those iced coffee drinks from Ingram's. Have you ever tried their—"

"Sonya?" He grabbed her hand. "Thanks for the tea, hon. But can I read the mail, please? It won't take long."

She shrugged. "Go ahead. . . . Anyway, the filbert cappuccino is dreamy. There's—"

"Alone?"

Sonya frowned and stood. "Of course. As usual. Dinner's at six. As usual." She walked out, the fading rhythm of her steps

9

creating a much slower tempo than before.

Brad sighed. He felt like a heel, but the tight knot in his stomach was growing with each of Sonya's nondescript words. He took a swig of the spicy tea, feeling an icy trickle through his chest. *Now for the mail. . .*

He tossed the first unopened piece in the wicker trash basket beside him. Junk. He wished he could do the same with the second piece, a bill. "Junk. Junk. Junk." A stack of three hit the rim of the trash basket and rebounded in. . .all but one piece.

"Brad?"

He heard her, distracted by the rebellious envelope on the floor. It read Bike Escapes.

Inside, it said, "Bike Escapes can wheel you out of your rut for five fun-filled days." He chuckled, then frowned, reading on with an embarrassing eagerness.

The brochure featured several trails, one of which was only a few hours south, in Missouri. "Once the path of the M-K-T railroad, the Missouri Katy Trail stretches from St. Charles to Sedalia. The 230-mile path follows the Missouri River, lined by towering bluffs. Tour groups lodge in quaint bed-and-breakfast inns located in historic towns. Escape from your typical vacation and truly rest. For more information, call. . ."

Two hundred miles on a seat the size of an iron? Hardly *rest!* Sure, Brad had dreamed of getting away before. He would wade through salty waters on a Florida beach or nestle in a cabin surrounded by the Rocky Mountains. But Missouri? He pushed the brochure into the trash with the other discarded letters.

"Brad?" Sonya called again. "What's the name of that lady at our church who has the candle store?"

"Sorry, hon. Don't remember." Too tired to remember.

Bike Escapes can wheel you out of your rut for five fun-filled days.

He tried to picture it—rocky bluffs, an effervescent river. Tingling muscles. Breeze running its fingers through his hair. Quiet. The idea was sounding better. Why not?

He dug the brochure out of the trash and traced the number

with his finger. After snatching the phone, he punched the buttons as fast as if he was calling his best friend.

"Good evening. Bike Escapes," came a measured voice.

"Hi. What's your tour schedule?"

"I'm sorry. This is the answering service. Bike Escapes' business hours are eight to five. Leave a message?"

Brad glanced at the wall clock. 5:20. "No. Thanks anyway." He hung up, sinking back into his bear-brown chair. Familiar food smells reached him. Usually delicious, they made his stomach strangely queasy.

Familiarity breeds contempt. Unfortunately, the phrase made more sense with every wedding anniversary. A few days away from this place could help him clear his muddled thoughts. What could he possibly miss? He didn't have to know the trip's details. His next call could be a reservation, not an inquiry.

But he wasn't one to make an impulsive decision, especially when the bank account was so highly involved. He had to be one-hundred-percent sure, and even this rare, enticing desire only put him at ninety-nine.

Brad slid the brochure in a pocket in the chair, grabbed his bottle, and headed for the recycling bin. As he neared the kitchen, the scent of tomato sauce and oregano became stronger. He peeked in the door.

Sonya sat at the faux marble kitchen table, erasing a mark on little Maggie's paper. The five-year-old swung her pint-sized loafers back and forth, back and forth.

Sonya stuck a pencil in Maggie's pudgy hand, squeezing the girl's fingers gently into place. "Now you try it." The tiny loafers came to a halt.

The little girl squinted at the paper, her face squinting, too. She closed one eye and looked up. "Show me, Mommy."

"Okay, punkin. Now look. . ."

Brad crept in, hoping not to interrupt their little lesson. No such luck.

Sonya and Maggie twisted their heads in one synchronized motion. Maggie shot him a grin, her top right tooth missing.

"Daddy! Hi, Daddy." She ran to him and threw her arms around his neck.

He felt spoiled by such a display of adoration. But he hoped she would never stop spoiling him.

In contrast, Sonya clinked down her pencil and said, "Susan Mahoney."

Brad slid Maggie down, letting go only after a light thud told him that her feet had safely made contact with the kitchen tiles. Brad gave his wife full attention, like a squirmy kid staring in the barber's mirror just before a haircut.

"Didn't you hear me?" Sonya said, one eyebrow raised.

"Yes. Susan Mahoney."

"Then why didn't you say anything?"

Brad sighed. "Was it a question?"

"Brad, you *know* that Susan owns the candle store. Why did you say you had no idea? I don't understand you lately."

Ditto. He fought the lure of an argument, but Sonya's furrowed brow stood as a warning sign. *Why does Sonya ask a question when she knows the answer?*

Shaking herself from a frustrated trance, Sonya called Maggie back for more mommy-daughter tutoring.

Despite Brad's frustration, he couldn't help but watch. Sonya tucked her golden hair behind an ear and gave Maggie guidance in an angel's tone. Her blue eyes sang lullabies. He had to admit it—she was still beautiful, even after these years. If only he could recapture an appreciation for her inner beauty that somehow lost its melody to the ears of his heart.

Maggie leaned over to watch her mother's demonstration. Sonya explained again. "Start your pencil at the top then go down and. . ."

Obviously not needed, Brad opened the oven to confirm his suspicions. Yep, lasagna. Full of sausage, mozzarella, and ricotta. Just the way he liked it.

"You're letting all the heat out," said Sonya, looking up from the paper. "Did you know that every time you open the oven, the food can take five minutes longer to cook?"

The hinges creaked as the oven door shut. He knew Sonya was just being Sonya—her words netted with trivia, just to hear herself talk. No mal– intentions. "Well, it looks good," he forced as a peace offering.

Brad chanced opening the fridge, and he scanned the shelves. The cold rushed out, losing intensity with each second. Hopefully, Sonya wouldn't remind him of her knack for salmonella trivia. He found another bottle of tea on the top shelf and popped the lid.

He headed back to the family room once more. Thanks to Sonya, he knew the lasagna would need five more minutes to bake, so he had at least five more minutes to wind down. He popped the footrest into place again. This recliner, his escape. Funny how things happened. Once a gift for Sonya, now a hiding place for him. And yet, so many aspects of this marriage ended up looking different than he assumed they would.

If only things could be the way they used to be. . .

At least here, in his chair, he could be honest, unguarded. And when prime time lineups showed no promise, this is where he would pray.

He retrieved the blue brochure, opened it, and blew out a breath. "So what do You think, God? Should I do it? Should I go? Not as a selfish move. I'm not saying that. . . . Okay, I admit it was at first, but now I think it could help all of us. Me, Sonya, even Maggie. Right?"

Yes, it could.

"It could?" He wanted reassurance, but he didn't expect the answer so quickly.

Just don't expect everything to be the same as it used to be.

Brad didn't doubt now. A green light was what he wanted. But for some reason, divine approval made him feel infinitely more uneasy about the whole idea.

two

Doing homework with Maggie made Sonya hungry. Almost everything made Sonya hungry. As she modeled the twenty-third letter *d* and wrote the names of a zoo full of animals, the kitchen timer announced the end of their study session. "Dinner, Brad!" she yelled toward the brown corduroy chair.

Strangely, tonight her husband did not come. Usually he arrived, unhurried but prompt, eyeing the entrée.

"Brad?"

"Coming!" he said, his voice sullied with distraction.

What's wrong with him lately? Every day he made a beeline to that stupid chair without so much as a hug. Sonya tried anything and everything to break through to him. At first she talked about things that mattered to her: how she felt lonely sometimes, how she hated that her dress size went up. But that only made him withdraw more. Now she resorted to insignificant conversation. Like names of ladies who owned candle stores. Why did he act like he didn't hear her anymore?

She scoured the counter to pass time. Still no husband. "Brad!" She wadded the dishcloth and tossed it in the dishwater, then marched to the family room.

He was still in that disgusting chair, the footrest up, reading something—a blue brochure. Actually he wasn't reading it, just staring ahead at what appeared to be nothing but the wall.

"What's that?" Sonya asked, pointing.

Brad blinked, not looking up. He tucked the brochure into the side of the chair, almost as a reflex. Then, much more slowly, he slid it out again, holding it low in his lap. "Oh, this? It's. . .um. . .I'm. . . Well, I'm going out of town."

She squinted at him. "Out of town? Why?"

"A bike trip across Missouri. It's only four nights. And—"

"For what?"

"For *me*."

What's that supposed to mean? "Who are you going with?"

"A tour group called Katy Escapes."

After a pause, she lifted her eyebrows. "I. . ." What could she say? She could either table this conversation or return to blackened lasagna. "Can we talk about this after dinner?"

"I need this, Sonya. I need a break."

"No denying that. Come on." She leaned, yanked down the footrest lever, and went back to the kitchen.

Sonya carried the baking pan to the dining room table and jabbed a metal spatula through the layers of steaming noodles.

"You hungry, sweetie cakes?" she called to Maggie, who was scribbling in the kitchen.

"Yup!" the little girl replied, getting up. *Like mother, like daughter.* Sonya put a portion on the little one's plate, too.

Brad finally joined them, lips locked as usual. "Here," Sonya said, handing him the spatula. She'd made the meal á la Brad: extra cheese, stuffed with ground sausage even though she liked it differently, thank you very much. Did it matter to him?

Brad slid the spatula under a piece. As he lifted it to his place, it slid into his lap.

Sonya gritted her teeth. "Sorry, Brad." She stood, flapping her hands helplessly. "Can I help you? Do you need a towel or maybe the trash can? Oh!" The words tumbled out. Though she frequently used long strings of them, she rarely felt like she communicated adequately. She rarely felt heard.

"Sit down," said Brad a little louder than usual, but not much. He already had the big pieces off his lap.

He's mad at me. He didn't act it, but she knew. He had to be.

"Be back," he said, and left, wiping the sauce from his sweats with handful of flowered napkins. Almost everything in a two-foot radius had an orange tinge to it now.

"Mommy, can I start my dinner?"

Oh, Maggie. Sonya knew her five-year-old must still be hungry. No reason to fault her for that. "Yes, yes. Tell God thank you and go ahead."

Maggie clasped her stubby fingers together and bowed her head.

How precious. Sonya marveled at what a sweet little girl she had. The two were joined at the hip from the time they stopped being joined at the umbilical cord.

Brad came back in a pair of jeans. He stood up to serve himself this time, holding his plate over the baking dish.

"Are you soaking your pants?" asked Sonya.

"Let me guess," Brad said, frowning. "If I don't soak them within three minutes, the stain will set, and they will be ruined forever. Am I close?"

She was just trying to help. Trying to fix the mess she caused. She nodded, "Yes." She tried not to ask again, but couldn't resist. "So did you?"

"Yes," muttered Brad. He bit at the tines of his fork thoughtfully then scooped up another portion of pasta, which landed square center on his plate this time.

For a few minutes, a conversation-void meal amplified the lonely sounds of forks clanking against plates and water sloshing out of tumblers.

"How was school?" Brad finally asked his daughter.

Eagerly, Maggie rambled about a video on spiders she had seen at school that day. Sonya absently cleaned her plate. How she wanted another piece. Especially after the spill incident. Whenever Brad was angry with her, she felt a huge hole inside. Maybe not in her stomach, but close enough.

"I'll have one more sliver," Sonya announced, almost as if asking permission. Brad had wadded his napkin already.

The piece she lifted was smaller than the first, but it felt like it weighed a ton. Just like her. For the last several years, the pieces of lasagna had joined cookies and colas to wage war on her hips. Brad's eyes followed the piece from the tray to her plate. *He wishes I wouldn't eat it.* Did she correctly detect his embarrassment when they met up with his friends? Did he want to hide her pudgy body with his fat-free physique? Not that she was obese. She fell within her weight range. At the top. For now.

Brad said, "Excuse me," and left. The sound of clapping came from the other room where Brad had undoubtedly taken charge of the remote. Game shows.

When Sonya's eyes focused again on the table, she noticed Maggie cutting her leftover noodles into lopsided geometric shapes.

"Ready for your bath, punkin?"

Maggie put down her fork. "Can we do the bubbles?" Her squeaky voice sounded full of them already.

"Yep. I'll meet you in the bathroom in one minute."

Maggie's dangling feet hit the ground, and she was off like a comet. Sonya swallowed. She felt full. But she cleaned her plate anyway.

After clearing, rinsing, and loading the dishes, Sonya headed toward the bathroom. En route, she stopped when she spotted the blue pamphlet in Brad's hands again. She pasted on a smile as best she could and sat on the family room love seat. She breathed a prayer before she spoke. *Dear Father, he probably does need a break. How can I fault him? It would do us both good.* She took a deep breath and asked, "Okay, what is this Katy Trail?"

Brad muted the television and actually looked at her. "It's on an old, converted railroad track along the Missouri River. I'll stay at bed-and-breakfast inns along the way."

Sonya had only dreamed of staying at a bed-and-breakfast. She subscribed to antique magazines, and though she never read any of the articles, she soaked up the photos of lace-adorned rooms until she knew which one came next before even turning the page. Brad didn't know eyelet from organza. What in the world did he want with that kind of vacation? "I hear they serve the most delicious dishes. Juices and quiche and pastries and bacon." Her mouth watered. "Do you know anyone in the group?"

"No." He sighed. "Anything else?"

Yes. A lot more. Especially one thing. "Can I come?"

He looked at her as if her hair had fallen out.

She continued. "Well, why not? It sounds beautiful. I've dreamed of staying in a bed-and-breakfast for years. I'd love to have a room with a fireplace, and I'd die for a feather tick mattress. Have you ever slept on one? Really, I haven't, but I hear they're absolutely luxurious."

"Are you serious? We're going to be biking fifty miles a day, or more. This is going to be serious work, Sonya."

Yes, fifty miles sounded hard. Impossible. But maybe not, if she had time to work on it. "When is it?"

"I don't know." His voice had an edge to it.

"You don't know!" Suddenly, Sonya recognized the sound of water running. Maggie must have started running her own bath. She could imagine the little girl emptying the bubble bottle dry—and finding mounds of suds towering to the towel rack and beyond.

Sonya's voice sounder higher by the minute. "Do you have any idea what you're doing?"

"I'm looking into it." His eyes poured back over the brochure. "Face it, Sonya, you're in no shape to do something like this. You would be miserable."

Sonya wrapped her arms around her thickening waist, her dinner still heavy inside. Brad didn't think she could do it. He didn't want her to go. Her voice sounded like a little girl as she objected. "Honey, don't write me off as a lost cause yet." As a biker. . .or as a wife.

The water still rumbled.

"Coming, punkin!" Sonya studied Brad's chestnut eyes. Did they ever look at her deeply anymore? Maybe this bike trip was just what she needed to win back their gaze. She'd drop a few pounds, prove she could do it, and he would look at her again. . .the way he used to. If only she could convince him to take her along.

"Maybe you're right, Brad. . .maybe." But she didn't think so. And hopefully, after she followed her plan, he wouldn't think so anymore either.

three

"Guess it's about time I started training for that bike trip, huh?" Brad said one evening after a hospital TV drama. He peered from his corduroy throne; Sonya reclined on the love seat.

Sonya's limp eyelids opened wide. "Um, yes, I guess so. I. . . it's just that. . .well, isn't it too dark out? It's ten o'clock." She had a strange look on her face, like a kid who'd been hiding cookies in her bed.

Brad shook his head. "Not *now*, Sonya."

Sonya smiled weakly then closed her eyes.

An opportunity to dominate the conversation for once. "Let's see. The trip leaves in October. That's six weeks away."

"Seven," said Sonya, almost as if talking in her sleep.

Brad counted the weeks on his fingers. She was right. "Yes, seven."

His wife's head craned against the back of the love seat, loud breaths came from her open mouth. It was amazing how she could lay in such a contorted position and still look so feminine, so pretty.

In fact, lately he'd noticed that something was different about the way his wife looked. A good kind of different. But he couldn't put his finger on it. He examined her hairstyle and makeup, but neither had changed. She must have been trying a new skin care regimen or some other woman's beauty secret he didn't have the insight to discern.

At any rate, he liked what he saw.

Now Sonya slept, unaware of Brad's tender stare. For a moment, he felt guilty about going on the bike trip without her. She'd asked to go along, but he'd convinced her she could never make it. When it came to Sonya breaking a

19

sweat, walking Maggie to the bus stop was second in line only to vacuuming the living room.

His guilt abated. *No* was the only practical answer. They both knew it.

Brad closed his eyes and began to drift off with visions of tire spokes and gravely roads. It was his turn to dream.

❧

The next morning, Brad trudged out to the garage wearing bike shorts and a tank top. It was early September, warm by the afternoon, but he shivered as the cool morning air tickled his skin. He lifted the garage door and rolled his bike backward through a maze of boxes and tools. He sat down, and—

"What?" When Brad put his foot to the pedal, his knee almost bopped him in the nose. "Who adjusted the seat?"

The bike repair shop; that's it. Brad admittedly hadn't taken the bike for a spin since he'd gotten it adjusted and oiled weeks ago. They must have greased the seat bar and left it down.

Brad hopped off and adjusted the seat to a comfortable height. Suddenly, another strange sight caught his eye.

Mud. Dried-on mud. *No explanation for that.* He flicked the dirty clumps off and sat down. Again. He finally sent the wheels to spinning and cleared the driveway.

The morning sun had cleared the two-story houses of Driscoll Lane, and the breeze brought goose bumps out in Brad's bare arms. He pedaled faster, hoping that his working muscles would warm away the bumps from the inside out.

As Brad started up the first hill, his mind wandered to the Katy Trail. He'd pedal on part of the "Rails to Trails" project. Crushed limestone paths covered the ground where wood ties and iron rails once carried train cars. He would surely speed along on a flat trail like that. In a few weeks, he would be there, on a pleasure trip. By himself. He imagined Sonya and Maggie home while he indulged, and sullen guilt rose up again. But then the thought, *Will they even miss me?* Too often he simply felt like a third wheel in his own house.

Wheel. He'd have to buy a spare tube and bike kit soon.

Brad's goose bumps continued to grow, despite his rapid pedaling. He did a 180 and headed back home. By the time he reached the driveway, he'd gone five miles, and hadn't broken a sweat. This trip was going to be even easier than he thought.

four

Two weeks later, Sonya pedaled a cherry red twelve speed into Cosmic for a limeade. A young carhop carried out the icy drink on a plastic tray. Sonya paid, took a sip, then looked around. She knew that she couldn't possibly be the first person to have pedaled into the drive-in restaurant on a bike. But suddenly, she felt silly balancing on the bike seat while two husky men scarfed burgers in a towering Jeep in the next spot. Sonya rolled the bike over the curb and sat in the nubby grass to finish her drink.

Home was a post office, a grocery store, and three lofty hills away. Sonya fastened her helmet straps and shoved off to make the final leg of the training run. The cool liquid in her body gave her a second wind, and even the menacing hills failed to faze her.

It was one o'clock when she finally caught sight of the familiar ivy-green garage that she'd closed three hours earlier. Lunch waited, but Sonya felt no urgency. She reveled at odometer numbers that boasted *28.7*. Two more than last time. By the end of October, she should easily be ready to take on the Katy.

The garage door clamored as she lifted it, and she rolled the bike back next to the Christmas tree box. She wished the seat wasn't so narrow, but what could she expect? It *was* Brad's bike, after all.

Not owning a bike posed an apparent problem for the trip, but Sonya had thought of that weeks ago. In St. Charles, where the trip would begin, several bike shops offered rental service. The morning the tour shoved off, she would pick the model, the color. . . It would be just like buying a new sweater from the mall.

Sonya smiled. As odometer distances had gone up, the numbers on the bathroom scale had gone down. Even if joining the bike trip somehow backfired, Sonya had something to show for all her hours of hard work. Actually, *less* to show.

A scale didn't need to tell her that her chins turned from two to one, and her bike pants no longer fit like a tourniquet. She had wondered when Brad would notice and compliment her on the return of her lost figure.

She still wondered.

Sonya wiped her sweaty brow with her shirttail and turned to head back to the house. She was still thirsty, her limeade tank now dry. A cold glass of—

"Brad!" Sonya tripped backward and caught her heel on the kickstand. She began to fall, but her husband's firm grasp acted on impulse.

He pulled her to her feet and looked at her, then the bike, then back at her again, blinking. "Sonya?"

"What are you doing home?"

"I forgot the—a better question is, what are *you* doing here?" Brad's eyes were wide.

"Um. . .what's it look like?" *My only hope. There's a one-percent chance he'll guess wrong.* Sonya might have been sneaky, but she wouldn't formulate an out and out lie.

"Well, this may sound strange, but it looks like you just got back from a bike ride." He lifted his eyebrows, making the statement into a question.

"Yep, that's what it looks like, doesn't it?" Sonya never had a shortage of words. Where were they now?

Brad bit his finger in thought. "So that might explain how mud appears out of nowhere."

Well, she'd guessed the odds of her discovery accurately. "Brad. . .let's talk. It's time to spill the beans."

"Just how many beans are we talking here, Sonya?" he asked.

"Oh, a kettle will probably do."

They faced each other in typical argument position: opposite sides of the kitchen table. Brad sat resting his chin on his knuckles. Not a good sign.

Sonya guessed she should start. "Well, that day I found you looking at the brochure on the bike trip, I asked you if I could go along, remember?"

His eyes bored into her; he must have thought it a rhetorical question. Sonya cleared her throat. "Yes. Um. . .I wanted to go, and you said you didn't think that would be a good idea. And when I asked why, you said because I could never do it. Well, I thought, if that's the only reason, then we'll just have to find a way to change that. So I went out to the garage a couple of days later, but your bike wasn't there. I think that's when you took it to—"

"Sonya! Make your point."

"Okay." She took a breath and clasped her hands together. "I've been training. For several weeks. And you were wrong, Brad. I *can* do it. I went more than twenty miles today."

Brad's face showed awe—at first. Then anger. "When were you going to tell me this?"

"When I knew for sure that I could make it."

He leaned back and folded his arms. His face softened. "I'm impressed, Sonya. I mean, I am truly amazed. But I have some bad news for you."

"What?"

"That trip filled up months ago. Only a half dozen people can go at a time, and—"

"Oh, that's not bad news," Sonya tried to temper her excitement. "I copied down the number and booked myself for your group."

"You what?!" Brad stiffened as his voice raised. "I can't believe you, Sonya! You knew that I needed to do something by *myself*." His fingertips thumped on his solid chest.

What don't *you do by yourself, Brad?* Sonya hung her head. Her stomach growled, and she craved the leftover cheese enchiladas from the fridge. She would even eat them cold, shoveling bites right out of the pan with a spoon.

"Sonya. Say *something*."

"What's to say?"

"I wonder that question every day, but you always seem to have an answer."

Sonya leaned forward and whispered. "Well, not today."

five

Brad covered the front desk at Area Gym, reading a news letter from Bike Escapes. Gear, locations, trivia. He read it twice. Once, as a man with a retreat in mind. Again, as a husband with his wife on vacation. He told her he still wanted to go solo, but too many words remained unsaid to reach a final verdict. And the words that were said. . .well, many of them would require penance.

A trim, balding man approached the desk and flashed his membership card. Brad nodded and smiled. Two more men walked by, flipping their cards in Brad's direction.

He turned away from the next guest, the flamboyant red-head who frequented the tennis courts. Instead of the other patrons' typical five-second-entrance, she put her elbows on the desk ledge and leaned over. Her scoop-neck tennis dress exposed too much of her freckled skin.

"Hi, Brad," the woman said in singsong.

"Hello, Erin." He pulled out the Katy Escapes letter and feigned reading it again.

"What's that?" she asked, pointing a glossy, brick red fingernail at the page.

"Well, a letter."

She leaned farther, her long hair brushing his face. "Katy Escapes? Sounds like a movie where a chick digs a hole through a prison wall or something." She giggled, making her hair swing back and forth. Then she stopped and said, "It's not, is it?"

"No." Brad felt his face flush. *Don't you have a tennis match soon?*

As if she heard him, Erin glanced at the clock. "Oops! I'm a little late. Tell me more later." She stood up straight and rapped the ledge twice with her knuckles. "See ya!"

"See ya."

Erin was the kind of woman teenage boys gawked at in magazine ads. Maybe in perfume ads, a laughing woman running with a tanned beau through the sand. Brad let his mind wander to a make-believe page Erin and he skipped across.

Suddenly Brad rebuked himself. With a hard blink, he tried to shake the image. *Sonya could be a magazine cover girl, too,* he reminded himself. Maybe one in a detergent ad, where the laundry and the model appeared clean and bright. When Brad had first met Sonya, she had the same kind of effect on him as Erin did. But unlike Erin, she wasn't trying; her magnetism just came naturally. Now what once was a magnet had turned to a thick, gummy paste that made him feel stuck.

It was that familiarity problem again, he guessed. What was left to discover about her? He'd seen her in almost every situation imaginable—at her best and at her worst, as the wedding vows had predicted. They had fallen comfortably in life's routines, almost able to prewrite life's weekly script with the aid of a few notes from the family calendar.

Erin, on the other hand, was a high-action movie preview. She revealed just enough to make men want to see the rest. But words like *commitment, devotion,* and *faithfulness* kept him from going there. He was resolute about it. *Not a chance. Really. Dear God, You know what I promised before a church full of friends and family.*

And yet, it made it that much harder to go home to nagging.

૨ન

After his shift, Brad jogged to the minivan he and Sonya proudly bought last year. Off the lot, brand new. Now, a throaty laugh alerted him that Erin was behind him. He slowed, embarrassed to get in the massive family-style vehicle while Erin watched.

He climbed in and put his forehead against the rim of the steering wheel. *Sonya. I love Sonya.* He pulled out a memory to

confirm it. It was the night she had said, "I'm taking *you* out."
She stood before him in a full-length gown with just enough
twinkling sequins to make her sparkle, without looking gaudy.

He had tugged on his belt. "But look! I'm in jeans."

And she said, "No problem. Your suit is laid out on the bed."
And sure enough, it was. . .

Knock. Knock.

That fist with the glazed nails was rapping on the van window to have the last word. "Bye, Brad."

Erin sashayed away with drama, as if she were Marilyn
Monroe in a tennis skirt.

Brad looked down and tried to picture Sonya in her gown
again, but all he could see was his wife in sweatpants, her hair
done up in a messy ponytail. Since Sonya started bike training,
that had become her uniform more often than not.

six

He's an hour late! Sonya cracked the oven door and peered inside. Petrified pork. Either dry or cold. A no-win situation.

"Mommy, will you play cook and clean with me?" This was Maggie's version of "house."

Sonya crouched, eyeball to eyeball. "Okay, punkin. Who are you today?"

"I'll be your mommy, okay?"

Sonya turned the oven off and followed Maggie to her room, to her elf-sized stove and baby bed. Maggie explained, "Now you come home from school."

They always started there. It was the place Maggie knew where to start. Did her family really know what Sonya did all day while they were in their own worlds, leaving her in one that belonged to everyone? Sonya put on a strained smile. "Mommy, I'm home."

"Hi, Punkin," Maggie said. "I'll get you a snack, and we can look at your papers." The little girl started for the play stove when she stopped in her tracks. "That made me remember something. A paper for you."

A drawing? a sticker for a job well done? Sonya smiled, unforced this time. They abandoned the fantasy house and emerged into the real one to their real responsibilities.

While Sonya checked on the dinner again, Maggie dug in her pack. She waved the paper at Sonya. "A permission slip. Sign it."

Sign it? No 'please'? Just assumptions. Mom is the hub of the family wheel. "Let me finish this first. Or have Daddy sign it when he comes home."

"Daddy?" Maggie said, as if she'd believed her father was illiterate.

29

"Yes. Daddy!" Sonya poked a pork chop with a fork. Might as well have baked a doormat. Suddenly she felt furious at Brad. "Can't you ever ask *him* for anything? Am I the only one who lives here?"

Maggie stumbled back a step, teary-eyed. "Right now you are."

Sonya's anger blinded her compassion. With an angry voice, she said, "That's right, little lady. And since he's not home yet, I suggest we go out. Put on your shoes. Dad can have an all-you-can eat shoe leather buffet when he comes home."

As Sonya went for her purse, she felt self-disdain. *Who was that ugly woman who just snapped at my little girl?* She sighed. "Come on, Maggie. I'm ready."

Maggie began to tie her shoe when her antennae went up. She shoved her foot the rest of the way in and ran off calling, "Daddy!" her untied shoelace flopping against the carpet.

Sonya followed. She knew where to find them. When she reached the two in the family room, Maggie had wrapped her arm around Brad's waist, and he patted her on the head.

Sonya said, "Brad. Welcome home, honey." *Hear him out. Don't go for the jugular. . .yet.*

"Hi." He looked down.

And? Why are you late? Sonya wanted to ask, but she knew that once they came out of her mouth, her neutral greeting would deteriorate into angry words. Her anger would stir his, and she hated when Brad was mad at her. She hated it even worse than her own anger. *Let him bring it up.*

Maggie ran to her room and came back with the unsigned permission slip. Sonya said, "Oh, I'll sign that."

"No, don't you remember, Mommy? You said, why don't I ever have Daddy do anything?"

"I. . ."

"Here Daddy. *Do* something." She put the permission slip in her father's lap.

"Don't do anything, huh?" Brad asked, pulling a pen out of the chair's side pocket. He clicked the top emphatically as he peered at Sonya from the tops of his eyes. After they met eyes, he scrawled his signature.

Sonya wanted to deny her words. To say, *Maggie is young; messages got crossed in that undeveloped mind of hers.* A little fib would have been easy to throw together. But trust reigned over comfort. Sonya stuck with the truth, just backpedaled a bit. "No, that's not what I meant, Brad. You do a lot. Just not as much as I would like when it comes to. . ." She pointed to their daughter as if Maggie didn't understand.

"I'm working, Sonya."

And she wasn't? Hey, he even got paid! She tried to sound matter-of-fact as she voiced her proof. "What about Sunday mornings before church? I've got roasts to stick in the crock pot and my hair to roll and Maggie to get ready, and you read the morning paper until it's ten minutes to go while I run around like a chicken with its head cut off."

Sonya huffed. Brad tensed. No progress. Time to change the topic. "Maggie's class is going to the rodeo for her field trip. I went with my Uncle Tim when Mom was in the hospital. I remember the horse exhibition when—"

"When's dinner?" Brad cut her off, reclining like a king in his corduroy chair.

Sonya had given him his chance to apologize about coming home late. *Time's up, buddy.* She answered with faux cheerfulness, "Oh, whenever you want. You won't believe what we're having tonight."

Brad looked at the far wall. "What?"

"Be glad to, Brad. 'Cause you'd never guess in a million years. I think it used to be called pork chops and roasted vegetables, but now I would just call it garbage."

That got his attention. "What's that supposed to mean?"

"It means that you're so late, it died on me."

"Sorry, Sonya." *Here it comes. Better be good.* "One of my clients stopped me. I kept telling h. . .him I was late, but it wasn't sinking in."

Sonya put her hands on her hips. "I get tired of that story.

You were off the clock over an hour ago. Just tell them you're done for the day."

Brad gritted his teeth. "It's not that easy, Sonya. Stop meddling in my job. You don't understand."

"I *do* understand that it is more important than coming home on time to be with your family. But then again, what isn't?" *Good comeback. That will make him race home tomorrow with an armful of flowers, won't it?*

"You don't know. You have no idea!"

"That's the truth." Sonya turned away, tearful. She wanted to cry out to heaven, but she breathed a silent prayer instead. *Dear God, I can hear myself, but I can't stop. I feel so much anger pouring out of me, but I have already said too many words I regret. Help me, Lord.*

Brad lowered his voice. "I don't think it's a good idea for us to go on this bike trip together next month. Why put my hard-earned money toward a four-day, sixteen-hundred-dollar argument?"

"You've got that right, Brad. You should put that cash toward an eight-hundred-dollar escape, just like the brochure says. And as for me—I'll just stay here in this prison while—" She had to stop to ask God for much-needed self control. Again, a silent prayer. *Father, help me stop. No more. Brad's got the point. I'm sorry. I'm sorry.* Sonya collapsed on the love seat and folded her arms. "Maybe you're right, honey. Go on the trip by yourself. It won't change anything around here. But maybe it will change you."

"It takes two, Sonya. I'm not the source of all our problems."

"I didn't say that, Brad." She was tired of arguing, so she said, "Just go, okay?"

Brad's eyes softened. "Maybe we can find a bed-and-breakfast to stay at in November."

"Yeah, maybe." *A bed-and-breakfast guilt offering. Did that mean mission accomplished?* Sonya wasn't sure whether to feel happy or sad. She knew God's desire was to prosper the marriage, not to see it come to harm. Why did her mind seem blank after times like these?

Brad wandered off, and Sonya heard clanking dishes in the kitchen. Her husband called, "This doesn't look so bad, Sonya. We can at least make these veggies into minestrone with a can of beans and tomato soup."

All that frustration for nothing. Or was it?

❧

Sonya stepped out of a dressing room that smelled of five different brands of perfume. She turned, hands overhead, wearing a turquoise dress that dripped with tags. It was gorgeous, with a tapered waist and scoop neck. She said, "I don't know. . . I already have a dress this color."

"You look beautiful in it, dear. You could be a teenager again." Mom always knew how to relieve guilt from overspending.

Sonya turned to the full-length mirror. "Have you noticed I've lost weight?"

"How could I miss that? And what reward have you given yourself? Buy it."

Sonya checked the price again. A little steep. But. . . "I do love it."

"How much did you say that bicycle trip cost?"

"Eight hundred."

"Well, now you have eight hundred dollars to spend that you didn't have before."

"I thought you said I should go on the trip," Sonya said.

"Did I say that? Oh, get the dress. It will last a lot longer," her mom said, with a flick of the wrist. "You deserve it."

Sonya hugged her mom. "You convinced me. Sold." *Eighty dollars down and $720 to go.* Actually, Sonya had no intention of spending that much, but she did see the reasoning behind a little more frivolity than usual. "Let's try the shoe store after this, okay? I need shoes that do justice to this dress."

❧

Sunday morning, the alarm roused Sonya from sleep at her usual time. Normally, she left Brad sleeping in bed for another half hour, but that day, he got up with her.

"Why up so early?" Sonya asked, throwing on her bathrobe.

"I'm going to *do* something," he said.

"What are you going to *do*?"

"Don't you remember? 'Daddy doesn't do anything.' I'm going to change that notion this morning. Leave Maggie up to me. You do your roast and your hair thing." He waved his hands in circles over his head.

The crusty veggies didn't seem so tragic with the dawn of the new morning and Brad's gesture to help out. But Sonya had unexpected misgivings about his plan. "It's okay, Brad. I was in a bad mood last night. Let me take care of it, and you go back to bed."

Brad shook his head. "Sonya, don't say things you don't mean. Let me do this or don't mention it again."

After some thought, Sonya said, "Fine. The punkin's all yours for the picking."

Brad went to the kitchen for breakfast, and Sonya stepped into the shower. She began to lather her hair when she heard a child's cry. Instantly, Sonya twisted the knobs, double-handed.

Silence.

After perking her ears up for a minute, Sonya resumed her shower. Showering was one of her favorite moments of the day. A time when the pulsing water and her uninterrupted thoughts joined the music of her echoing voice in song. But this morning, even with all this extra time, she couldn't seem to be present. She went back to the bedroom with a knot in her stomach.

At the closet, Sonya flipped through the fall wardrobe that had just come out of hibernation. She pulled a pine-green twin set over her head and her pants up to her waist. When she buttoned them, she almost had to sit down in shock.

Maggie could have fit in the pants with her. Well. . .maybe they were not *that* big; but almost.

Sonya tossed the pants to the floor and pulled another pair off their hanger. Same loose fit. The pile grew as Sonya's wardrobe dwindled. For once in her life, she took pleasure in having only half a closet full of clothes, which were mostly tops.

After settling on a velvet dress with a back clasp, Sonya began her hair. She had three rollers left when—

"No!" This time, the child's cry was not an illusion. "I like the red one!"

"But it's too cold for that one." Brad's voice sounded strained.

"But Mommy *always* lets me wear that one."

With clumps of hair draped between rollers, Sonya sped to Maggie's room and threw open the door. Brad stood holding an assortment of dresses with clothes littered around his feet. He looked like he was being burned at the stake.

"Mommy!" Maggie ran to her the instant she saw her. "Daddy's not letting me wear my red jumper."

"You do what Daddy says, young lady!"

The little girl jutted her bottom lip and stomped her foot.

"Mag—gie!"

"Okay."

It took every ounce of Sonya's strength to retreat back to the bedroom, and it seemed as if no amount of foundation could cover up her weary-looking eyes. *This is worse than if I'd done it myself.* The protests and orders continued, and she wished she had gone back to bed and had a low-key nightmare.

Twenty minutes later, the voices quieted, and Sonya ate a bagel as she pulled the giblets out of the Sunday chicken. Brad and Maggie walked in to heat up some oatmeal.

"Oh, Brad!" Sonya cried when she got a look at her daughter. "What's this? Her barrette is on sideways, and her hair is sticking out in every direction. Did she even brush her hair?"

"Did you brush your hair, Magpie?" Brad asked.

"Yes. But I couldn't find my brush, so I used my doll's."

"Ugh! Punkin, go get my brush from the vanity," Sonya said. She tied the chicken's legs together, and as she yanked the knot she said, "Brad, what is she wearing?"

"Is that really bad? You should have seen what she wanted to wear!" He laughed.

"It's not funny. She needs to change. I don't want people thinking that our child is a poor orphan." Sonya rinsed her hands and shook the water from them. "Let me finish her up, okay?"

Brad's jaw tensed. "Yeah."

❧

The weeks that led up to the bike trip tasted bittersweet. Sonya and Brad were actually civil to each other. Brad tromped in the door late more often than ever. Sonya held her anger in more often than ever. She tried to act as if everything was normal, whatever normal meant.

She tried to convince herself that all husbands ignored their wives.

But then one morning, Sonya woke up and saw Brad crouched over two suitcases, and one was hers. "You've worked so hard for this," Brad said when he noticed her eyes had opened. "Harder than me. Sunday morning, all I had to see was that sermon title, and I knew what was right. Got your suitcase. . ."

"I. . .don't know what to say." Sonya was wide awake now.

"I still want time to myself, Sonya. If you say yes, please remember that."

That moment could possibly mark a new beginning. Or a beginning of the end.

seven

Brad continued to pack as Sonya sat up in bed and stretched. He thought about his pastor's sermon. *Grace is giving forgiveness that we don't deserve. Love that we haven't earned. It is the life of Christ ending on a cross when He did nothing wrong. It isn't fair. But it is right.*

It would be fair to leave Sonya at home after her deception. But it wouldn't be forgiving or loving. It wouldn't be right. Brad decided to take the idea a step further, for good measure. "When I'm done, I'll get Maggie packed."

Sonya sat up, threw back the covers, and jumped out of bed. With a forced smile, she said, "I'll do it. Don't bother."

Yeah, I'll probably pack the wrong hair ribbon. Why even offer? With clipped words, he said, "If you say so."

"I'm trying to be nice," she answered, throwing the door shut behind her.

That was so typical for Sonya lately. Any time Brad didn't reply with the right tone or the right words, she pouted and became silent. It was almost worse than her monologues. Yes, she had been eerily quiet lately. Granted, she did ask him occasional questions like, "Did you get the oil changed?" or "What do you think about my new tennis shoes?" Questions he'd rather not answer.

And then when he said something like, "I'll set up an appointment with the lube shop as soon as I can," she always had a follow up question.

"Next week? Next month? After the engine block cracks?"

For the most part, she put on a smiling face and did so well at acting that Brad wanted to nominate her for an academy award. Every once in a while a little steam would puff out— like with the oil change interrogation.

Brad paired some sports socks, rolled them together, and threw them in the corner of his suitcase, hard. The pair bounced completely out. Brad took a deep breath and gently put the runaway socks next to some others.

The moment of motivation to pack had passed.

Brad pulled himself to his feet and flopped down on the end of the bed. He couldn't get his mind off Sonya. It triggered strained feelings that were now coiled, ready to spring at the smallest incident.

Marriage wasn't supposed to be like that. Tension around every corner. Assumptions that spoke louder than Brad and Sonya's true voices. The feeling that Brad resisted being with the one person he'd vowed to love and cherish forever.

And yet, Brad could admit that he was not simply a poor, innocent bystander to a roly-poly wife who smelled of pepper and brandished a rolling pin. He had been staying at Area Gym too late some nights.

Of course, Sonya was even more perturbed when Brad walked in late and dinner was not up to restaurant quality once again. She finally waited for him to come home before she put the ingredients in the pot. Which only made the three hungry family members even crankier.

Brad could admit that he rarely asked Sonya how she was doing anymore. And he told her how he was doing even less frequently than that.

Yes, Brad could admit his mistakes to himself, but if he ever told Sonya, he was afraid his words would be nothing more than a death wish. Afraid that every time they had a problem she would use his admission as proof that he was entirely to blame.

Now Sonya's sweet voice seeped under the closed door. Maggie's squeaky voice followed. Brad couldn't decipher the words they said, but Sonya's tone said love and interest and patience. The woman who spoke was the Sonya he married years ago. She *was* still buried inside.

With that reminder, Brad felt certain of two things. One, he knew he still loved his wife. Two, God had an infinitely better design for their marriage than their current situation.

And now Brad and Sonya stood on the verge of this monumental bike trip. Maybe it was just what they needed to clean their slate and start anew.

But just how much scrubbing would it take to clean it? More than a few incidental days on an old Missouri road?

And once the slate was clean, what would they write on it?

&

The basics stacked neatly into Brad's suitcase with room to spare. He relinquished the family's cargo-sized suitcase to Sonya, and she still asked if she could put her hairdryer in his. Women!

He put the bags together like a puzzle in the back of the minivan, with just enough room for Maggie to buckle up on her way to her Aunt Leslie's house where she would be staying.

On the road, Sonya navigated Brad to St. Charles with a fold out map. As he pulled up Riverfront Drive into the trailhead parking lot, his minivan joined another vehicle. Anticipating meeting the others, he was suddenly grateful that Sonya sat beside him. She could befriend a person of any persuasion in just minutes, while he just talked about the weather.

The other vehicle, a long navy van, hogged several parking spaces as it sat sideways with a trailer in tow. It vibrated with the beat of the music that pounded inside.

"Wait here," Brad told Sonya. She nodded, unusually quiet, and played with the straps on her bike helmet. Was she having second thoughts? Even though he still felt uneasy about her intrusion on his getaway, he felt oddly protective of her, too. If she couldn't make it, he wouldn't shove an *I told you so* in her face. He would feel bad with her.

Brad reached the van driver's window. "Hello!" Inside reclined a broad-shouldered, broad-necked black man with a shaved head. His eyes were closed as he played his steering wheel like a drum.

Brad pointed at the stereo buttons, and the man took the

clue as he popped out his CD. Suddenly Brad could hear the chirp of birds he didn't know existed. "I'm looking for the Bike Escapes group."

The man leaned back and swept his hands out, palms up. "Look no further."

A feminine voice behind Brad startled him. He turned to find a lady, probably in her fifties, with the body of a thirty-year-old, reached out her hand. "Are you Hank, Brad, or Amir?"

"Brad." They shook hands.

"I'm Judy McCoy, Bike Escapes trail leader. And that's our supply wagon driver, Fletcher."

Brad looked over the woman with new eyes. She stood a little over the five-foot mark, her brunette hair in a neat bob. *Our leader?* Not that anything was wrong with her, but he had expected someone like. . .well, like *him*.

"I see on your info page that you work at Area Gym in Springfield. It will be good to have a fitness instructor on the trip," she said. "I admire those who have the discipline to go to a gym on a regular basis, but I prefer to get out in wide open spaces. You know the saying—to each his own."

"Yeah, that's the saying." Brad repeated. "That's what they say—"

"Wow! I am so excited about this trip! This is gonna be awesome." A short carrot-topped man broke in. Or was he a kid? He was in that in-between stage where a male's voice had stopped changing but his laundry pile never made it back into the dresser drawers.

"Hank?" asked Judy, shaking hands again.

"Yeah, baby!" Hank grinned from ear to ear. "When do we start? I'm ready, all right." He shuffled on his feet like a boxer. A lightweight boxer in the skin and bones division.

"Not yet. I take it you had a long drive from Louisville, huh?" Judy asked.

"Took the bus. I slept most of the way. Now I'm rested up and ready to blaze this trail."

"You live in Louisville?" Brad managed.

"Live? I guess you could call it that. I go to University of Louisville. I'm a freshman."

"What's your major?" Judy asked.

"Hmm. Let's see. Currently, I'm majoring in scarfing down pepperoni pizzas at midnight, getting ninety percent of my sleep from naps, and trying to find a girl who will look at me. But if none of those work out, I guess I'll do computer programming."

Ugh! Brad gazed off in the distance. He had more in common with the fifty-year-old bike leader than this lanky college kid with no apparent direction. But they would be on the trail for the next few days. Brad figured he probably wouldn't have to spend much time with Hank at all.

Judy said, "We're waiting on one more couple, then we'll go over the itinerary."

"Gotcha," Hank said, pointing at her with both hands.

Brad looked back at his car. When he caught Sonya's eye, he motioned for her to join him. She swung open the door, stepping out on new, bleach-white jogging shoes.

When Sonya reached Brad's side, he put his arm around her waist. He was actually starting to feel relieved that she had come, feeling unsettled in the midst of this mismatched gathering.

"I'm Sonya," she said, reaching out a hand to Judy, then to Hank. "It's great to meet both of you. I was wondering who would be our partners in this trip. I imagined an army of buff men on huge bikes. And me—trailing behind with rubber legs."

"Oh, no. This is a vacation, dear, not boot camp. You will love it!"

"I'm already seeing that." Sonya looked at the vibrating van. "Is he one of our group?"

"Yes, that's Fletcher."

Sonya shot a twenty-four tooth smile, raised her hand over her head, and waved as if she was bringing Fletcher in for a landing. The driver incorporated a few return waves as part of his imaginary drum rhythm.

Judy put her hand over her brow, scoping out the road. Hank rummaged through a U of L bag that was branded by a fierce cardinal logo. But Sonya didn't seem to notice. She kept making conversation. "Louisville? I've never been there. . . . Did you all have breakfast? We weren't sure what to eat. A lot? A little? We ended up splitting a farmer's breakfast at a little diner. . ." The disjoined words kept flowing, but Brad didn't hesitate to let her carry the conversation.

"Looks like we're all here now," Judy finally said, pointing. A BMW skidded in, followed by a white cloud of exhaust. Out stepped a dark-haired, olive skinned man in black bike pants. From the passenger side came a woman with thick, raven hair in a side part. They looked slightly older than Brad.

"We made it," said the woman, laughing, her diamond-studded hand resting on her husband's shoulder. "Fashionably late, as usual, but we made it."

"Audra and Amir here," said the man, extending his hand. He had a slight accent that Brad couldn't quite place.

Judy shook it and checked her clipboard. "I see you're veteran bikers. Between you and Brad—who's a gym manager—I don't see why you need me." She laughed.

Amir said. "Experience helps, but it's not a substitute for a great guide."

"Well, thank you," she said, the laughter ebbing to a flattered smile.

Audra added, "We just bike for exercise, not competition."

"But this week it will be a vacation," Amir said, looking at Audra. He took his wife's hand and kissed it.

Audra pecked Amir back on the mouth, unaffected. She tossed her hair and turned back to the others. "Well, everybody, tell us about yourself. Who are the rest of you?"

"Hank here," said the carrot-top.

"I'm Sonya. I'm glad to see I'm not the only female. Do you know—oh, I'll ask later. Nice to meet you."

Brad followed suit.

"And Fletcher, our SAG wagon driver," Judy intercepted.

"Yo," said Fletcher.

"Except he doesn't like the term. He'd rather we referred to the van as the Happy Wagon."

"Sweet!" Hank, of course.

"What's 'SAG'?" asked Sonya.

Judy explained. "Supplies and Gear. It's all in there, with lots of food and limitless water. Fletcher will meet us at each trailhead to help us refuel our bodies and troubleshoot problems." She turned to Fletcher. "Can you pass out the info sheets?"

He nodded and passed a yellow paper to each participant.

Judy continued, "You should have received these already, but let's look them over again. Questions?"

Audra raised her hand, wiggling her fingers. "I was wondering, how did each of you come to be here?"

Amir pulled his wife close and kissed her on the cheek. Brad started tapping his foot.

Judy answered, "Audra, you will have hours and hours to get to know everyone—you'll see." *Good answer, Coach.* "Anything else?. . .All right. Our first SAG. . .er. . .*Happy* Wagon stop is in Defiance, Daniel Boone's town.

"Marthasville is our final destination, thirty-nine miles from here. Remember, it's vacation, not a race. Take it as slow as you want, and you speedy bikers, listen up; never lose sight of the guy behind you. Let's go!"

"Woo hoo!" Hank cheered. And the seven vacationers broke out of the circle in every direction.

Minutes later, Fletcher blasted his music again and pulled onto Riverfront Drive, leaving the group with their bikes and whatever few possessions could fit in a small bag.

❧

Brad noticed numbered markers announced each mile pedaled. *These can't be right! They reflect only four miles so far; twenty-five more to go.* Sure enough, his trusty odometer confirmed it. But his tight legs told a different story.

Sonya pedaled next to him, her mouth working as persistently as her legs. ". . .and then the checkout girl forgot to scan the coupon. After all that, can you believe it? Why did I even bother to go back home? Sometimes I. . ."

The couple had a continual view of Judy and Hank. Audra's occasional giggles came from behind.

Five miles down; twenty-four to go.

Wasn't Sonya getting the least bit tired? If so, her voice sure disguised any fatigue. "Oh, look up there, Brad. The trees' colors seem perfectly mixed. Isn't it incredible?"

"Yeah," Brad answered.

"Just *yeah?* Don't they just take your breath away?" Sonya shook her head in disgust. It was as if she always had to convince him to be as happy as she was.

Brad sighed, then added, "Pretty. Yes, they are."

Sonya paused, then whispered, "Don't pander to me." She rose on her pedals and sped up a few feet in front of him. At least she stopped talking long enough for him to hear the breeze rustle and the geese cry overhead. Reminders that there were more than six of them on that leg of the Katy Trail. An unspoken reason why he had come.

In the day in, day out life of work and errands, TV reruns and family meals, he couldn't seem to tune into God much anymore. Jesus retreated to the desert, the mountains, the shores. Could these Missouri bluffs become Brad's sanctuary? "Will You speak now, Lord?" he whispered with a catch in his throat. "I know You're there. I see You in the clouds; I hear You in the birds' cries. I feel You all around me. So listen to me, please.

"I love Sonya, but sometimes she can be so irritating. She traps me in a suffocating box and wonders why I yell to be let out. Detachment, as You know, has been my answer. But I know that's not Your best for us.

"I am still angry that she tricked her way into coming along, but I want to move past that. I forgive her, Lord. Please help this trip to bring us closer to Your ideal for a love-filled marriage. Even if it means some growing pains."

Not having heard a word, Sonya dropped back next to him. "I didn't mean to upset you, Brad. I just—"

"I know, Sonya. I know. Forget it." He took a breath. "I love you, hon."

"Love you, too." She cracked a smile and on the next breath began, "Hey, did I tell you what Mom found out last Saturday? We were. . ."

But as far as growing pains go, God, the lighter, the better. Brad glanced at the sky, and suddenly he knew God had been listening from the start. All along, it was Brad who truly needed to listen.

eight

A red-tailed hawk glided overhead. Sonya thought, *Well, hawk, I've always wanted to fly like you, and today, I feel as if I am.* The air brushed against her cheeks like the touch of a cloud, and her legs felt as if they could pedal all the way to the other end of Missouri.

Time seemed to move at half pace as she pedaled down the trail. In the course of a minute she could soak in the rich hues of sumacs and maples and bittersweets, hear the rush of the distant river. But when Sonya had remarked on the beauty of it all, Brad became aggravated. Even with the beauty surrounding them, Sonya thought he would appreciate having her commentaries to keep his mind off of the monotony of pedaling.

Another mile marker. Judy signaled to stop. "We've got about four miles left till we meet up with the Happy Wagon and get some lunch. Everyone okay?"

They all nodded.

"How about you, Brad?" Sonya whispered.

"Me? I'm doing great." He acted as if she'd asked a rhetorical question. "How about *you*?"

"It's easier than I thought. I'm not even tired."

"Great. I knew you would do fine." His eyes even sparkled.

Sonya's surprised heart danced. She wished she could kiss him right there.

They started again, two by two. "Did you see that water pack Amir had? It's like a backpack with a straw—the gold standard in water bottles. I wonder how much one of them costs?"

"I saw it, Sonya. I see it all." The sparkle had dimmed now.

"Well, okay." She decided to take Brad's cues, to be humble enough to realize that she did demand too much at times.

This time, she would respect his need. If he didn't want to talk, he didn't have to.

Sonya's attention went back to the golden trees. All unique, all asymmetrically perfect. Still, she couldn't keep quiet. *Someone* would listen. "God. . .Creator. . ." His name was a prayer in itself when murmured amidst the branches of this live autumn canvas. "I can't believe I'm here. Me, the one who couldn't resist an afternoon of craft fairs and lunch dates, now traveling miles on end on a bike. It goes to show that nothing *is* impossible with you." She smiled. "Even the possibility that Brad and I might live as soul mates again. Please, God, use this trip to meld us back as one, as You desire. Our relationship once seemed so right. When did we begin to drift?"

They *were* soul mates, once. She knew it the afternoon they met at Monaker Pool. Twenty-two-year-old Brad smelled of coconut as he sunned on a beach towel. Blaring music traveled through his earphones, so loud that he might as well have not been wearing them at all.

Sonya tapped him on the shoulder.

He smiled and put the headphones around his neck. "Hi. Everything okay?"

"Yeah. . ." She swallowed and said, "That song; it's one of my favorites." Contemporary, yet spiritual and deep, this music had touched her heart. "I'm Sonya."

He put the headphones aside and rolled over to face her. He smiled, but said no words, just looked ready to hear whatever she had to say. Sonya didn't remember much of what came out of her mouth that day, but she couldn't forget the look in his eyes that said, *I'm listening, and I'm interested.* Or his tender manner—not acting like he had to prove himself.

Sonya didn't want to seem too forward, but she couldn't just let this young man come and go like a wispy dream. Other men would gawk at her (in those, her beauty years), but Brad showered her with respectful admiration. She couldn't explain how his compliments had been different from other men's, but they were. They were.

He began to gather his belongings when they both began to ask a question at the same time. "You first," he said, stopping.

"No you." She was curious.

"Not many people would have recognized this Christian artist's music. But you not only know it, you were bold enough to say so. Do you come here often?"

I do now!

※

At the little town of Defiance, the group met up with Fletcher. The big man undid the trailer's padlock and lifted out a cooler as if it were empty, which was hardly the case. Judy and he passed out tall drinks and clear, plastic boxes loaded with cold food. Sonya bit into a plump strawberry and knew that a piece of almond cheesecake (her favorite) couldn't have tasted any better at that moment.

Everyone found spots along some wooden ties and greedily dug into their boxes. Sonya lifted a foot-long sub out of the box, then looked at Brad.

She was hungry. Not like the impulsive cravings that used to enslave her, but a healthy hunger that said she'd burned a warehouse of calories already today. With closed eyes, she bit in, the hearty flavors satisfying her taste buds. She immediately took another bite without hesitation and without guilt. That is, until she opened her eyes again, noticing Brad staring at her.

Audra and Amir leaned against each other on their railroad tie, soaking sun like June time. Serenity smoothed their faces. A vacation brochure expression.

It's what Sonya came for, too, and a much-needed sandwich wasn't going to rob her of it. Sonya remembered her old youth pastor's words. "Associate with those you want to be like." So she turned her attention the way of the couple.

Amir had finished a sip of his drink, and he was saying, "It's hard to believe anyone is working this very moment. It seems so contrary to reality."

"*I'm* working," Judy said, with a laugh.

"You are a wise woman," Amir said, "to get paid to sit in the sun."

"So what's your profession, Amir?" Judy asked.

"Real estate. I started with residential, but now I run my own commercial realty. The AFK Group."

Sonya swallowed her next bite. "Didn't you rebuild that sky-scraper after the arson fire last year?"

"Yes, how did you know that?"

"I saw it on 'Wake up America.' That's one thing I'll miss this week—my morning cup of cinnamon tea with the latest news blinking before my eyes. I feel handicapped if I go a day without an update."

"Too violent for me," Audra countered. "I like the human interest part, but when blood enters the picture, I get queasy. Amir fills me in on the big news. . .minus the doom and destruction."

Sonya nodded. "I'm not into sensationalism either. But see-ing the problems of the world makes mine seem so small sometimes. At least for one hour of the morning."

Brad slid his arm around her. It felt moist and warm and welcome. He said, "I wouldn't know what was happening out-side Springfield if it wasn't for Sonya. And she's telling the truth; she's not into sensationalism. But she writes congress-men and rounds up donations. All kinds of acts that make a difference to the community, even the country. I wish I had her passion, her compassion."

Sonya leaned away from Brad to get a good look. Could he have said that much to a stranger? And about her, no less!

"Impressive," Amir said.

"Thanks," Sonya said to Amir, then looked at Brad. "Thanks, both of you."

Suddenly Hank came running toward the group. Had he been gone? He went to the open trailer and took out his full box of food. "Hey, this place is awesome! Did y'all know that Daniel Boone and his wife settled down here in 1799? They had two hundred and fifty great-grandkids. Can you imagine?"

"Like rabbits," Amir said, and Audra laughed.

"What did they do about Christmas presents?" Sonya added. Brad laughed deeply and gently elbowed her. "A white elephant gift exchange, no doubt." Their smiles met; white elephant gifts were a long-standing and hilarious tradition in Sonya's family.

"That might take all twelve days of Christmas, Brad," Judy said, standing. She turned. "Fletcher, can you lock back up?"

"Yep." He went to toss his trash—two boxes and a root beer can.

"Hey, where'd he get the root beer?" asked Hank, a bit of lettuce hanging out of his mouth.

"Mine," Fletcher answered, crushing the can in his hand.

"No problem," chirped Hank, and he took a swig of his lime sports drink.

28

The sandwiches and strawberries and sun gave new life to the group's depleted muscles. At a nearby café, they topped it off with ice cream. The seven journeyers filled three different checkered tables as if they didn't know each other, except when Audra stopped to chat on the way to wash her hands. Sonya was still full, but Brad bought an ice cream crunch bar and offered her a bite. She accepted, not because she wanted any, but because she saw it as a gift—something that said he was thinking of her.

After the six licked the last wooden sticks clean, they hopped back on their bikes and sped off, quickly becoming old friends with the trail. Sonya and Brad talked about a magazine article Sonya read, Area Gym's new whirlpool, and how their living room curtains needed to be replaced. It was the longest mutual conversation they'd had in ages. No brown chair to provide escape. No child's squeaky voice to demand attention. Only open air with no overpowering background noise. Sure, Brad's words were few. But his attention span was gaining ground.

Now for the big league. "Brad, I was thinking about us and—"

A skidding sound broke off Sonya's words. Her adrenaline rushed. She swerved as she turned to look in the sound's direction. Brad's blurred figure fell at the mercy of his bike's whims. He had gotten too close to the shoulder, and his bike's wheels slid on the chalky chat and over the edge of the trail. He toppled over his bike into some overgrowth.

"Judy! Wait!" Sonya immediately yelled, shaking, and the others stopped and jogged back to them.

"What happened?" Judy asked, panting.

"Looks like Brad was trying to imitate a stunt double," Hank said.

Sonya gave the facts.

"Here, friend," Amir said, offering a leather-gloved hand. He pulled Brad to his feet and brushed gravel pieces from his back.

Brad slapped his leg. "I can't believe I did that. My calf had a cramp, and I just lost control. Now look." His pants had ripped along his ankle, and blood seeped through the fabric. "It burns like lightning."

Judy worked the pant leg up with care, but Brad winced. She said, "Fortunately, Augusta is not too far, and Fletcher can fix you up with the first aid kit. Being a former football player, he knows how to wrap just about any body part with expertise."

Sonya went to Brad's bike and wheeled it back on the path next to her husband. She said, "Honey, I'm glad you're okay. When I saw you go down, I thought it was a good thing you had your helmet on."

"That fool helmet didn't do much for my throbbing leg," Brad said, frowning.

"Could be a lot worse, Brad," Amir said.

"Yeah, thanks," he said, nodding.

Sonya gritted her teeth. He seemed much more accepting of Amir's words.

Then she realized the awful truth. She'd distracted him. That had to be it. Brad had brought her along on his vacation, and now he was on the sidelines while she kept pedaling. All because of her.

nine

The searing pain in Brad's leg hurt less than his crushed ego. After Judy and Amir examined the cut, they concurred that it had missed all tendons and shin bones and that perhaps Brad would even be up and biking again by tomorrow.

After one rotation of his bike's pedals, Brad knew he could not complete the half-mile to Augusta. The weight of his body on his cut calf made the pain shoot. He squeezed his brakes to a halt and tipped the bike, standing on his good leg.

"What's wrong?" Sonya asked, stopping, too.

The others circled back again. Surprisingly, their faces held concern, but Brad couldn't believe that was what they were really feeling. They paid for a vacation, not a first aid frenzy.

Brad explained his predicament to Judy, not Sonya. Judy was about to suggest an extreme measure, such as finding a bike-trail version of a Saint Bernard when Amir held up a hand. A grade school gesture, but it stopped her mid-sentence. He said, "I can help." Amir dug out a gadget that looked like a pocketknife and tossed it in the air.

"No amputations, please," Brad said, hoping his comment was nothing but a joke.

"That was plan B," the olive skinned man said with a half-smile. He pulled a fixture from the pocket knife, which didn't end up being a pocketknife at all. Instead, various tools were folded in the case. Amir crouched down, inserted the tool in his pedal, and twisted.

Judy stuck out her bottom lip and nodded as if she understood. After applying the tool to both pedals, Amir held two metal devices that resembled mouse-sized bear traps. "Here," he said. "Try these."

"Toe clips?"

"Yes. You can almost bike one-footed with these." Now Amir crouched next to Brad's bike. "May I?"

"It's a nice offer, but maybe I can make it after all," Brad said, feeling like a beggar.

"Brad! You take those. . .toe thingies!" Sonya ordered. "Amir went to a lot of work to get them off. And you need them."

Brad's mind formulated an angry sentence with the phrase "Yes, Mother" in it. But he held his tongue and froze up.

"Your wife loves you, Brad," Amir said. "Listen to her."

"Okay," Brad said. But not because of Sonya's pleas. "I'll try it. How nice of you."

Amir attached the left clamp and said, "Audra and I are glad to share almost anything. Just don't run out of water. No one drinks out of my straw."

"My husband's Mr. Generosity," Audra said. "But also the most hygienic. He says cleanliness is next to godliness."

Amir made his last twist, and after he stood, Brad shook his hand. "I'd say generosity is even closer to godliness. Thank you, man. May God give you an extra jewel in your crown for your kindness."

After a shrug, Amir said, "I'm not sure how all that works. God and our good deeds and all, but I accept that as a thank you."

Brad had made the comment part tongue-in-cheek, but Amir's remark made him stop. "Well, I agree," he said. "No one knows how it all works. It's said that our lives here are like looking through a glass dimly at who God is. But, I am learning more and more with certainty as time passes. My dim glass is letting in a little more light as time goes on—as Christ shines through." He cleared his throat. "That's…that's my experience." Brad hoped he hadn't come on too strong, but it wasn't as if he had even decided to say those words. They just came naturally, and heartfelt. Amir seemed to be an upstanding citizen type. Someone who could change from a spiritual ambiguity to a personal connection with the Living God. Maybe this would be all Brad would get to share during the trip. Maybe, somehow, God could use him to speak further to Amir.

The awkwardness forced him to look away, and he met eyes with Sonya. Her face was fixed in a proud, unbelieving expression. She raised her eyebrows and flashed an approving grin. For a few seconds, he forgot about his calf, the pain. But soon enough, the others' waiting eyes reminded him.

Brad plunged a rubber sole into the borrowed toe clips. His good leg pushed in hefty down strokes and used the toe clip to pull up when his injured leg took its turn bearing the weight. With the added crutch, he could survive the half mile.

After a grove of trees approached view and then disappeared, sounds of changing gears became the only communication among the bikers. Brad could feel the heat rise in his face. He felt beet red, though not from exertion. From embarrassment. He had fooled himself into thinking that gym managers were like Superman. Invincible. This was just another reminder that he was anything but. The self-assured Brad Kane was a fraud, toned but not trained. And after only a few hours, everyone on the trip had discovered the truth, too. How else was he living like that—putting his faith in a label, not a lifestyle? Was he like this in his spirit too? Could the words of a double-minded person hold any credibility for Amir?

❧

A navy blue speck in the distance eventually transformed into the Happy Wagon, parked outside a bike shop. Fletcher leaned against it, eating a candy bar. Brad was so relieved, he wanted to hug the man, but didn't dare.

Judy called ahead, "Get the kit, Fletcher. We've already got a casualty."

Fletcher stuffed the remaining half of the candy bar between his jaws, waved, and disappeared to the rear of the trailer.

Brad sat on the rim of the van's oversized tire as Fletcher wiped and dabbed, clipped and wrapped. Sonya ran her fingers through her husband's hair as shooting pain proceeded throbbing.

"Hey, can we sign it, Brad?" Hank asked.

"It's not a cast, Hank," Judy answered.

Audra said, "I say we sign it anyway!"

Brad leaned over protectively. Half smiling, he said, "No one is touching this leg."

"I don't blame you, Brad." *Thanks, Amir.* The dark-eyed man continued, "Judy, do they have lube oil in that bike shop? My brakes are squeaking."

"Oil, bike parts, sodas, snacks. . .basic stuff."

Gravel crunched under Hank's feet as he darted for the trailside shop.

Judy laughed. "They have a bathroom, too."

Sonya kissed Brad on the forehead, then followed the others inside. Brad touched the spot on his head, still moist from the kiss and perspiration. He watched Sonya walk farther and farther, admiring the tightening curves in her legs, until she disappeared inside. Would she would be joining him in the wagon soon, unable to finish? In a way, he hoped she would.

He situated himself in the shotgun seat, and Fletcher pointed to the long, vinyl seat behind him. "Want the back?" he asked.

"Thanks." Brad took his advice. As he propped up his dud leg, Fletcher turned the key in the ignition. Simultaneously, the engine and the loud music revved up, and the van pulled out. Brad gritted his teeth. *Ugh! Too loud.*

As if reading Brad's mind, Fletcher clicked the clamoring speakers off. *Finally!* After a minute of silence, Brad asked, "How many years you been doing this?"

"Two."

Strangely, Brad found himself initiating conversation. "That Judy seems like a dynamo. You two get along pretty well?"

"Tight," Fletcher said, and he popped the tab on a root beer. A twelve-pack sat half-empty at his feet.

Brad raised his voice to compete with the root beer fizz. "I hear you played football. What position?"

"Tight end."

"Why'd you quit to drive a SAG wagon?"

Fletcher eyed him in the rearview mirror. "*Happy*—"

"Oh yeah. . .*Happy* Wagon."

"Torn ligament," Fletcher said, in response to the question.

"That's tough," Brad sympathized.

" 'S okay."

Brad could get used to this. Fletcher was his kind of conversationalist: laid back, to the point, somewhat detached. But this detached man resurrected his music with deafening discord. Brad involuntarily cupped his hands over his ears. *Then again. . .*

With nothing else to do, he pictured Sonya biking solo on the picturesque path with only nature's quiet music to entertain her. She had been so sweet, the way she got his bike for him, how she became teary-eyed at the sight of the gash, how she kissed him on the forehead like his mother used to when he got hurt.

Too bad he felt too angry at *his* misfortune to enjoy Sonya's gestures at the time. Or to let her know how they made his heart smile.

"How many more miles left?" Brad yelled over the bass.

"Eleven."

It would be a long hour.

At least Brad would have time to think. Time to himself. Isn't that what he wanted in the first place?

Brad stared out one of the van's square windows. The scenery blurred past. He felt a twinge of guilt over leaving Sonya on the trail. And yet, Sonya had always been the more disciplined one. When they dated, she announced on Talk Radio 1020 before his alarm would buzz. Sonya, articulate and clever, sounding like it was already midmorning at 5 a.m. (The few times he was up that early.)

He had been so button-busting proud to be dating Sonya Foss. Just the memory made him wish himself back by his wife's side. Even if Fletcher's CD player had been playing Chopin. But she was pedaling and he was reclining, and that would not change until tomorrow morning, if then. With nothing to do but think, Brad's mind returned to the past. To the time when a crush became a commitment.

After a year of dating, Brad had popped the question. On their first anniversary, Maggie announced her beginning through a bout of morning sickness for her mommy. But even as a stay-at-home mom, discipline still thrived in Sonya; she scheduled delicious meals and kept the house clean. A professional nanny wouldn't have been more disciplined in caring for their daughter. But Sonya also spent money as if they still brought in two incomes.

Especially with her mom. Sonya's two weaknesses were money and family. And talking, of course. But just being out of a mall's reach gave Brad a sense of relief. No mother-daughter shopping sprees. No credit card receipts. Just Sonya and Brad. But actually, at the moment, just one miserable Brad.

ten

When Sonya came out of the bike shop, the van's parking spot was empty. The five bikers gathered, sipping water and zipping change back into their pouches. Sonya ran her fingers over her pouch: durable blue fabric sewn together with double stitches. Brand new as of five minutes ago, marked down 10 percent. And it matched her rental bike perfectly.

Sonya moved her older, dustier bag to a crook under her seat and put the superior one in its place. Though temporarily gladdened by the new purchase, she felt a hollow pocket in her happiness when Judy instructed them to move on.

Only Brad was gone, but somehow it felt like half the group was missing.

Hank must have noticed Sonya's lonely eyes. He tapped her on the shoulder and said, "Why don't you team up with Judy? I'll go solo."

"Are you sure? Thanks."

Hank hollered, "You hear that, Judy? I'm the leader of the pack now." He put a foot to the pedal.

"Sounds great, Hank. You can do some of the legwork for me. I'll take advantage of your back draft."

Hank pulled onto the trail. Amir and Audra fell behind, as usual, with Judy and Sonya sandwiched in between. Judy's back draft idea had a flaw, however. Hank, now solo, delighted in the full width of the path, weaving childishly from shoulder to shoulder.

Judy murmured under her breath. "Oh, to be young."

"How old *is* he?" whispered Sonya loudly enough to be heard over the tires' crunching.

"Twenty, tops. Lots of life ahead of him."

Sonya looked at the trail leader. She must have succeeded

where Ponce de León had failed in his quest for the fountain of youth. "You, too, Judy," Sonya said, "at the rate you're going. I was so impressed that you would be our guide. I guess age is only a number."

"Hey, now. I'm not *that* old!"

Sonya raised her eyebrows. "I—I don't think you're old at all. Just older than I am."

"I'll forgive you," Judy said, smiling.

Sonya liked the woman already. She hoped that they would have time to talk other days, too. Up ahead, Hank must have gotten dizzy because he'd started following the worn line in the trail.

"Are you married?" Sonya asked.

"I was. Tim died two years ago," Judy said.

"I'm sorry." Out of the corner of Sonya's eye, she saw Judy dab her nose with her sleeve. "You okay?"

"Mostly. But you're never completely okay. You assume you've got thirty good years left, and *bam!* All of a sudden, you don't even have a tomorrow. . ." Judy's chain clicked as her gears shifted. "Tim was a wonderful guy. He put up with my thirty simultaneous priorities. I hope he felt like he was number one. I competed in—or rather completed—mini triathlons every chance I got. During training periods, Tim would take over the cooking and the laundry as I ran, swam, or biked after a day at my desk."

Sonya blinked. What consolation did she have to offer Judy? "He sounds like he loved you a lot."

"A lot." She sighed. "At least the thirty years we *did* have were full of fond memories."

Sonya felt a tug at her spirit. "I'll pray that you will feel God close to you those times you miss him." Even now.

Judy jerked to look at Sonya so quickly that Sonya almost lost her balance. *Did I offend her?*

But Judy said, "Sonya, thank you! It seems we share something more than athletic ability. God has been my rock. He will help me stand firm long after this body does."

First, Sonya had to chuckle at Judy labeling *her* as an athlete. Then she thanked God for His sustenance—and for giving her a leader who knew Him as she did. "I look to God when I'm down, too, but I need to depend on Him more often. . . . If you don't mind me asking, how did your husband die?"

"An aneurysm. Quick and unexpected."

"How horrible."

"Yes. I thought I valued our times when he was alive, but I never thought I could miss him this much. The night he died we had just gotten back from buying toothpaste. He spent his last hour alive walking store aisles as I deliberated over gel or tartar control. It seems so stupid now."

They had been in the same place but heading different directions. Like she and Brad almost every day.

Judy continued, "Who could have known? At least I had no regrets when he died. Regrets would be worse than his death, in my opinion."

Please don't say that. Sonya had lots of regrets when it came to Brad. She regretted that they didn't have more fun together, laugh more together. She regretted that she nagged him more than she wanted to.

She regretted that she couldn't make him happy.

As if Sonya had said the words aloud, Judy remarked, "You have a nice-looking husband."

"I've always thought so."

"When I first saw you two, I thought, 'What a striking couple.' But you probably hear that all the time."

Sonya coughed, speechless.

"I'm sorry he had that tumble," Judy said.

"That's sweet. Thanks. Me, too." Brad's leg bled, but what was that compared to a bleeding brain? Brad was distant, but at least he wasn't absent forever, like Tim. A glimmer of hope stayed alive, too.

Hold on to that glimmer. Did Sonya think the words? They seemed to come from a voice that traveled in the breeze.

Judy continued. "Fletcher works magic with his combinations

of salve and bandages. Just watch."

"I hope so. Brad's looked forward to this trip for months."

"And you?"

"I didn't let myself. I wasn't sure I was going; I wasn't sure I could do it."

"I would have never guessed it. Most of the people who take this trip seem less prepared than you."

Sonya laughed under her breath. "Let's just say before this trip came up, my most exercised muscles were in my mouth."

"Well, don't neglect those either. I enjoy talking with you."

Audra hollered up to them. "How are you ladies doing up there?"

"Great," they said in unison.

Audra got out her "question pick" again to break some more ice. "Where are you two from?"

"Springfield. Illinois, not Missouri," Sonya said.

"St. Louis."

"Amir and I are from Pakistan, but relocated to Mission Hills, Kansas years ago."

Amir clarified, "And no, we don't have cows in our backyard."

Judy called back, "Amir, don't worry. I'd never have associated either of you with a cow. Or any barnyard animal, in fact."

"Forbid it," he said and took a sip of water.

"How many trips have you led, Judy?" Audra asked.

"Well," she paused. "About thirty. We average one a month."

"What's the strangest thing that ever happened on one of these trips?" Audra probed.

Judy told a story about predatory mosquitoes that followed them the length of the trail and back. "We started naming them. And having an insect bite competition we called, 'Who's the sweetest?' "

"I'm glad I wasn't in the charter group," Amir said, straightening his glove.

Audra continued her ten point quiz on the most unique aspects of Katy Trail. Hank began weaving again, oblivious to it all.

Dutzow was next in just four miles. When the bikers arrived, the Happy Wagon was nowhere in sight. Sonya had looked forward to seeing how Brad fared, to tell him she had dominated the trail. Her confidence had grown with each mile marker.

"Four more miles," Judy said. "We gonna make it?"

"Yes," Sonya said. *I'm going to make it. Thirty-eight miles. Who would have dreamed? And Brad will be there to see me cross the finish line.*

eleven

Brad and Fletcher waited at the Marthasville trailhead. A huge grain elevator to the right advertised Winery, in vertical letters, and the main street was just a bottle's throw away.

The two men leaned against the restored train depot, sipping water they'd drawn from the trailer's cooler. According to Fletcher, they shouldn't have much longer until they saw the others.

A speck approached. *Sonya?* No, it was an older gentleman on an older bike—manufactured in the days when multiple bike gears were as whimsical as an astronaut walking on the moon.

Brad's nose followed the trail back in the direction from which his wife should arrive. Shortly, another speck appeared. An unmistakably red-haired speck.

Sonya must not be far behind. On second thought, maybe she is. Maybe she's run out of—

But then came a brunette speck next to a blond one, bolting at full trail speed. *Well, what do you know!*

Hank rounded the corner and stopped next to Fletcher with a melodramatic skid. "We're here," he panted.

Brad stepped forward to greet his approaching wife. A faint pulse in his leg reminded him of why he hadn't finished the day's ride, too. He had to admit it; he was impressed that she hadn't called upon the Happy Wagon as a means of transportation at all. Brad said, "Sonya, look at *you!*" He smiled.

"Can you believe it?" Sonya glowed.

"No. I—" Brad was about to say something like *am so proud of you.* But an unfamiliar blue bike bag was attached to Sonya's handlebars. "What's that?"

"I bought it in Augusta. Isn't it great?"

63

"But you already have a bag."

"I know, but I thought I could carry more stuff this way. Maybe even a brush. I can't believe what this does to my hair. Judy calls it helmet head. I just call it plain ugly."

Oh, no. . .the ghost of my max-out-the-credit-card-mother-in-law. I was hoping she had stayed at home. "How much?"

Sonya put her hand over the bag as if protecting it from him. "Thirty. It was on sale. Ten percent off."

"Thirty! Sonya, I only brought fifty bucks!" Suddenly Brad was aware that five other faces looked his way.

"Sorry, Brad." Sonya hung her head.

Amir peeled his gloves off as he stepped toward them. "Brad, if you need any more cash, I can lend you all you want."

Brad took a deep breath as indiscreetly as possible. He said, "I appreciate that, Amir, but that's not the point."

"But you just said—" Sonya began.

The faces still encircled them. Brad whispered, "Let's talk later. Okay?"

"Yeah," Sonya answered, tears starting to well.

Brad felt a mix of emotions. *Oh, Sonya!* It wasn't that big of a deal. But she needed to understand that she couldn't buy every pretty bag that came along on a 10-percent-off impulse.

Judy cleared her throat and raised her hand as if to say, *Here! I'm the main attraction now.* She announced, "I have been with enough groups to predict a good trip. You all put your feet to the pedals and never looked back. And I don't think a single complaint polluted this fresh Missouri air today. Bravo."

Amir raised an imaginary glass. "Hear, hear."

Judy continued. "But we're not done yet. Killer Hill—as coined by the Marthasville natives—awaits."

"Bring it on," Hank cheered.

"We're in this together," added Audra.

Almost all of us, brooded Brad as he followed Fletcher back to the van. The two men led the procession to their night's lodging—Lavina's House-and-Breakfast. The group continued until they reached the bed-and-breakfast's driveway, the last hill of the day. They filed in the van's sliding door bringing with them the smell of dead leaves and expired deodorant. Sonya wouldn't look at Brad.

Audra tapped him on the shoulder. "How was your afternoon?"

Should he give the polite answer or the truth? "Great," Brad chose. But he felt like saying, *Can I get a refund?* "What now?"

Audra said, "Judy and Fletcher are checking us in. Then it's dinnertime."

"No showers?"

"No. We voted. Food beat out cleanliness."

Amir held up his hands. "Don't blame me, Brad! You know how I voted."

❧

The Happy Wagon rode its brakes down Killer Hill, smelling of burnt rubber and sticky bodies, and pulled in front of a small building. A sign hung in front with "Pat's Place" painted on it, undoubtedly a mom and pop operation, which was fine with Brad.

The crew went inside and huddled at the entry. A few locals dotted the tables, looking as if they had been there for a while and weren't in any hurry to leave. They gave the fleece-covered group a half-interested look then continued talking. As they chatted, they did not confine their conversation to their own tables like Springfield's chain restaurants; they hollered gossip across the room.

A young woman stepped forward, wearing an apron loaded with pens. "Hi, Judy. I see you've brought us another bunch. We're ready to watch the food bar get wiped out again tonight. . .and you, Fletcher, we're gonna charge you double, I think."

"Don't tell her about me," said Hank.

"Oh, you're one of *those*, too, huh? I wouldn't have guessed it, but the size of a body doesn't always predict the size of a stomach. Learned that years ago."

Audra suggested that they pull a few tables together, and as soon as they did, each grabbed a plate and started piling on chicken fingers and potato salad.

"Anybody have any kids?" Brad let Audra set the topic.

Sonya perked up. "Yeah, Maggie's six. And you?"

"Oh yeah. Four. Allen, Austin, Andrew, and Alicia."

"Well, I guess you can't label things with your initials!" Sonya laughed.

Brad caught himself smiling and imagining a tribe of Michaels and Melissas to add to his Maggie.

"Yeah, I assigned them numbers instead. Sounds cold, but it works. What's Maggie look like?" Audra said.

"She's got curly hair, and right now she's missing a tooth, but that will change. The teeth, not the hair. She has long eyelashes that would make any woman envious, and dimples."

"Sounds cute."

Sonya didn't answer, just gazed absently, seemingly fixed on ketchup splatters on the wall. She spoke in monotone. "Um. . . excuse me."

The metal feet on her chair screeched as she got up. More chicken fingers, Brad assumed. The apex of the current conversation shifted to Hank and Fletcher. Brad listened with amusement as the glutton brothers compared their calorie consumption and tried to one-up the other.

"Brad, where did Sonya go?" Audra asked a few minutes later as she swiped a fry through a puddle of ketchup.

Brad looked toward the row of cooking fuel burners that kept the fries and meat from turning waxy cool in their catering pans. A little boy rummaged through the onion rings. but Sonya was nowhere to be found. Brad scratched his eyebrow. "The bathroom, I guess."

"Outside."

"She went outside?" Now Brad's curiosity was piqued, and he was a bit worried. He scooted out his chair and went out to find her.

After exiting the diner, Brad scanned the Marthasville streets. They were empty, with CLOSED signs hanging in the shop windows. Brad finally spotted his wife a few buildings down holding a pay phone.

He looked both ways (out of Springfield habit), then crossed the sleepy road. Sonya wiggled her fingertips in a dainty wave but kept talking into the phone. "Is that right, punkin? And then what did the dream dragon say?"

Brad tapped Sonya on the shoulder. "Maggie?"

She nodded. "It's just about time for you to be meeting that dragon, don't you think? Have your pj's on? Good girl. . . Hey, guess what? Here's Daddy." She handed him the phone.

"Um. . .hi, Magpie," Brad said, thrown off guard.

The little voice on the other end sounded even younger than her six years. "Hi, Daddy."

His heart melted. "Well. . .how are you?"

"Good. I had macaroni and cheese tonight."

"Yum! I had chicken." Brad cleared his throat. The silence became louder by the second. "You do anything fun today?"

"Yep. I had lots of fun with Aunt Leslie." *No dream dragons to tell your daddy about?*

"Fantastic! You be good now."

"Okay, Daddy. Now can I say bye to Mommy?"

"Sure," Brad said. Sonya held her hand out as if she knew.

The two talked on, this time evidently about homework, while Brad stood by, watching the earthy rainbow of fall leaves fade into monochrome with the sun's disappearance. Along with those colors, the sun sucked down the day's warmth. Brad shivered. He hadn't brought his jacket; he hadn't planned on staying outside so long.

Sonya made kissing noises in the phone and hung up. "It was good to talk to her," she sighed.

How could she be so self-centered? She wasn't a single parent; there were two of them. Brad tried to think of something civil to say, but nothing came to mind. Instead he began a barrage of questions. "Were you planning on letting me in on the conversation? Or did I have to wander out by chance to get a turn at talking with my daughter?"

"Talking to Audra about our kids made me crazy. I just had to see if she was okay," Sonya said, with a surprised look on her face.

"And so you were just going to leave me out of this? Mom scores points while Dad gets another plateful of chicken, is that it?" He knew it wasn't. It was just that he was on the outside again. And it hurt.

"No, Brad. I just called Leslie to see how she was doing. Then Leslie put her on. Promise."

Brad felt his shoulders fall. "Well, okay."

"And I used the calling card. No more cash."

Don't remind me. He could see the bill now, another unexpected vacation expense. Not that he wouldn't have called if he went alone. Just not for thirty minutes.

Sonya rubbed Brad's arm, bringing a touch of warmth. "I'm sorry, honey. I'll tell you next time."

"Okay." He took her hand, and they headed back.

"So guess what Maggie told Leslie today? You'll think it's just precious. . . ."

❧

The Happy Wagon swayed back up Killer Hill, down the highway, and up Lavina's House's gravel incline, working a bit harder now that seven people's midsections had expanded from being filled to capacity. Fletcher pulled up to the main house, a 160-year-old farmhouse with a wraparound front porch. "You'll stay here," Judy said to Brad and Sonya. "In Aunt Lavina's room."

"Where's she gonna sleep then?" Hank laughed.

Brad winced. This little man's sense of humor needed serious fine tuning.

"Hank, you and Fletcher get Granny's Suite," Judy said, ignoring Hank's crack. "No questions about it," she said, fending off another. Hank's gaping mouth shut like a springed hinge.

"Audra and Amir, we put you up in that cottage," she pointed to a tiny building built of maroon-stained wood. "And

I'll be in the Pickerell room if anyone needs me."

Amir and Audra's dwelling, the Old Smokehouse cottage, used to be just that, a smokehouse. One would never know, however. Audra invited Brad and Sonya in for a two-minute tour. The rustic wood walls housed a mini two-story dwelling with a fireplace at ground level, and above, a snug loft for sleeping.

"I love this!" Sonya cried, scanning the evergreen walls, stopping her gaze at the natural stone fireplace behind a spiral-wound rag rug.

Though Brad agreed, he silently pleaded as he leaned against a padded chair. *Please, no more redecorating ideas.* Between craft fairs with her mother and magazine inspirations, Sonya kept their Springfield house in a continual state of pricey metamorphosis.

Brad followed Sonya back into the main farmhouse. Finally. They passed through an antique-laden living room and climbed the stairs to the guestrooms.

"This must be ours," Sonya said, peering in. "Oh, Brad! It's just what I dreamed." White lace decorated the dainty, rose-colored room, and a star-patterned quilt covered the antique bed.

Brad took a five-minute shower so Sonya could take a long, hot bath. As soon as he heard her water running, he stepped out into the hallway. There Brad found a nook featuring ceiling-high shelves crammed with old, hard cover books. Reading in a quiet room sounded like the pinnacle of the day—the kind of rest that had convinced him to dial Bike Escapes in the first place.

Brad tipped several books by their spines, glancing at the covers. He finally found a Norman Rockwell collection. Perfect.

After sliding the book from the shelf, he went back in the room, leaving the door cracked to let the bath's steam escape. The constant roar of pouring water suddenly ended, though the steam kept creeping out. He flopped down on the bed and opened to the first picture—"*Home Duty*, Rockwell's first Saturday Evening Post cover—"

"Brad?" Sonya's voice came muted through the door.

"What?"

"I am still amazed I made it today." He knew. She'd said it fifty times already.

"Yeah, good job," Brad said for the fifty-first time. *Back to Rockwell.* "This 1916 cover was the first of 324, an average of—"

"I can't believe how much you can get away with eating on this trip. But the funny thing is that I'm not all that hungry. Isn't that strange? When I was inactive, I wanted to get a vault for our junk food. Just lock it up with the temptation. I think they refilled the bin of chicken fingers at least four times at Pat's Place."

"Yeah, I was there, remember?"

"—an average of—"

"I wonder if Maggie is eating okay." Sonya opened the door and emerged in her pinstriped pj's, her hair wrapped in a thin, white towel.

I give up. Brad shut the book and rolled onto his back, lacing his hands behind his head.

Sonya continued, "I wonder what she's doing tomorrow? Leslie said they might go to that Peppercorn Puppets Theater, but I forgot which night. I think tomorrow. That place has the greatest special effects, I hear. I hope they don't scare her."

"Your sister is taking good care of Maggie. Don't even worry." Brad opened the Rockwell book again. As soon as he found his place, he heard a knock. Hank stood at the doorway with a frail book in hand. Definitely an offering from the tall bookshelf.

"Hi, guys." Hank held up his book and recited, "What can go up a chute down but not down a chute up?"

"What piece of fine literature are you reading, there Hank?" Sonya asked, rubbing her hair with the towel.

"*101 Riddles*," he said. "So?"

Sonya giggled. "I don't know. Tell me."

"I'll give you a clue," Hank said.

Brad could feel the tension rise in his chest. He just wanted a minute of peace and quiet; was that too much? Who cared what went whatever-which-way in a stupid chute? "I'll give *both* of you a clue," Brad said calmly, though he didn't feel calm. "I sat in the Happy Wagon with about twelve rap groups jabbering in fast motion today, and my brain needs quiet."

"No prob," Hank said with a smile, tapping the book on his palm.

"Thanks, Hank." This time Brad's tone was sincere.

As soon as Hank tiptoed off, Sonya grabbed her brush and pulled it through her hair. "Brad, lighten up. You're always too serious. He was just asking us to solve a little riddle."

"I'm sorry I don't appreciate kindergarten humor anymore."

"You don't appreciate *any* humor anymore."

Brad sat up. "You have no idea what I appreciate. You don't spend every waking moment by my side, listening to every conversation I have."

"Yeah, I don't spend many waking moments by your side at all," she said, now brushing her hair violently.

"I can't help it if my leg got jacked up today."

"I'm not talking about today, Brad."

"Look, I come home by dinnertime each night and eat with you and Maggie. I'm there to tuck her in when you need me to. I—"

Sonya threw up her hands. "You aren't listening to me."

"And you're not listening to me."

"What's new!" Sonya's limp, wet hair made her look more pathetic than threatening.

Brad walked toward the door. He turned and said, "Evidently not much. But I was hoping something might be different on this trip."

"Well, that makes two of us!"

Amazing. They were united in motive but totally disjoined in the effort.

Brad put in his last word. "Look. I know one way I can get some time to myself; I'll be back in a while."

❧

The night air bit through Brad's fleece jacket, but this time it felt refreshing. He felt hot from anger, but doubted that even Antarctica's climate could have given him shivers. Actually, he didn't know where he was going. He just knew he was going, and that helped him settle down a little.

The stars hid behind invisible clouds that made the night sky look a sordid gray instead of navy. To bad. He was sure the stars would shine twice as brightly here as they did in Springfield.

The light from Amir and Audra's cottage flickered. *Candles, perhaps? Logs crackling, spitting carbon flakes from the fireplace?*

A gust blew his hair and parted the clouds just enough for a few stars to break through. Sure enough, they gleamed with confidence.

"It's me again." Brad felt his chest tighten. "God, I admit I was in the wrong. But she. . .okay, no excuses. I'm sorry. Forgive me. And Father, please keep helping us get closer. It's what I want. It's what we both want. We're having a hard time figuring out how to get there. It was better today, but now this. Will it always be like this?"

Brad walked some more when he realized his leg hardly bothered him at all. He was only a few feet from the shed when he heard a clattering inside. *Raccoons? Thieves?* "Hank!"

"Brad. Shhhh!"

"What are you doing?"

Hank came out. "Shhh. We'll get caught."

"*We?* What will *we* get caught doing?" Brad raised his eyebrows.

"Glad you asked. Actually, this is a two-man job. It was providential you came." Hank explained his idea.

Brad shook his head, then turned to go. "I don't know about this."

Hank grabbed him by the sleeve. "Don't go. Come on, Brad. It'll be hilarious."

"No way." He kept walking, feeling his jacket stretch out of shape.

"Lighten up. You're too serious."

Sonya's words exactly. Brad sighed. "Look Hank, if anyone asks, I had nothing to do with this. Got me?"

"You bet."

Perhaps this could have an element of fun. It could help his emotions catch up with his prayer. "Okay, buddy. What's the plan?"

Hank laughed loud enough to wake Lavina's antiques. "Okay, since you have the big muscles, why don't you. . ." He whispered the rest. Then he said, "By the way, the answer is umbrella."

"What?"

"An umbrella can't go down a chute up."

Brad laughed. Perhaps the next hour with lanky Hank could be more enjoyable than a quiet night of Norman Rockwell.

twelve

The smell of ham and biscuits woke Sonya from a dream. She rubbed her eyes then pulled the quilt more tightly around her neck. Brad lay on the other side of the bed, his face sweet and innocent. His thick arm draped across her waist, and the warmth it brought instantly dissolved her cold dreams.

Yes, he had come back last night. She'd been so exhausted and her muscles so loosened by the hot bath water that even the echoes of the argument hadn't kept her awake—as they usually did. What time he returned, she didn't know. But his embrace said that he, too, had left their argument in the world of yesterday.

"Morning," she said, touching his cheek.

"Morning." Brad's eyes fluttered then closed again.

For a while, Sonya feigned sleep—a practice she used occasionally at home to ward off premature Saturday mornings. But Maggie wasn't across the hall to drag her out of bed. According to the clock, Sonya could do absolutely nothing for another twenty minutes. She closed her eyes and tried to convince sleep to wash over her again.

No! I don't want to sleep! They would only be at Lavina's House for another snippet of a morning. Her first bed-and-breakfast. She opened her eyes again and stared at the mauve-tinted walls, listened to the cooking sounds that *she* normally made. Her eyes traveled over the textures around her. The taut, smooth chair cover, flouting ribbons and ruffles. A netted table-cloth hanging in triangles from the corners of the nightstand. The early light making a soft reflection on the glassy lamp.

Springfield, Illinois, might as well have been Taiwan. And Maggie could be a fictional child heroine of one of the books in the hall. Sonya had landed in another world.

Even awake, twenty minutes of doing nothing went too fast. Sonya clicked the alarm off before it had the chance to do its obnoxious job.

"Brad?" she said softly, tousling his hair.

"Hmm?"

"This is your alarm speaking. I won't shriek if you won't sleep."

He rolled on his back and rubbed his eyes. "Thanks."

She kissed him.

Now his eyes stayed open, and he stared at her. "I'm. . .I'm sorry about last night. Hank was just trying to be friendly. I was tired and—"

"It's okay. I'm getting dressed. Breakfast won't be long." Sonya hopped out of bed and put on gray sweat pants and a zippered sweatshirt. She dragged a brush through her unruly blond mop. Brad sat and ran a hand through his matted hair and rolled back over. What a handsome couple they made! If only Judy could see them now.

Sonya dug through her duffel bag for a hair tie.

"Oh, my hair tie's in my bike bag." After Sonya said the words, she wished she hadn't. The bike bag. Another reminder of their squabbles. "I'll. . .just go get it."

Brad jumped up. "Your hair looks fine! Like you said, your helmet will mess it up anyway."

"What's with you?" Sonya whipped her jacket off the chair and clomped down the stairs. She passed Fletcher and Hank's room from which inhuman gargling noises vibrated the door.

Out the door and into the big yard. The clouds had cleared enough to give the sun a starring role in the sky's performance. Its rays highlighted the tree's leaves, making them almost seem to radiate their own colorful light.

Sonya walked along the drive to the shed. She pulled up the latch and swung open the door. Her bike was—

Gone! "Judy!"

Sonya ran in the farmhouse and banged on Judy's door. "Come quick!"

No one answered. "Judy?"

Sonya turned in time to collide with Hank who was pulling an aqua sweatshirt over his head. Sonya couldn't see his face, but she knew without effort that he couldn't be Fletcher. "Hank, have you seen Judy?"

"She's in the dining room," came a muffled response.

"Thanks," she said, leaving him to wrestle the sweatshirt.

As described, Judy sat in the dining room sipping a cup of hot tea, chatting with the hostess. Sonya stood next to her and described what she saw. Or rather, what she didn't see.

"That's strange," the hostess said. "We have never had any theft before."

"Thanks for telling me," Judy said calmly. She finished her tea. "I'm coming. Go get Brad, and we'll all have a little chat together."

Sonya found Brad upstairs, brushing his teeth. She grabbed his elbow and said, "Spit!"

Brad mumbled through mint foam, "Where are we going?"

"Judy's orders. Just come." Sonya dragged him downstairs and out the door. They found the whole group standing in the yard, facing Amir and Audra's cottage. Their mouths were all parted slightly, and their hands shaded their eyes from the morning sun as they peered toward the sky.

Actually, toward the roof.

There, on the cottage top, six bikes lay neatly stacked in an overlapping row. Sonya's face mirrored the crowd's expressions for a minute. Her blue bike lay at the bottom of the stack.

"Dude," Fletcher said under his breath.

"Who is responsible for putting our bikes *up* for the night?" Judy asked, her mouth quivering.

On cue, everyone voiced the same accusation. "Hank!"

"Why are you suspecting me? They're on *Amir's* cottage."

Judy said, "Try again, Hank."

"Okay. There was a tornado?"

"Good answer—if we were in Kansas."

"I give up," Hank said. "What is the answer?" *That seemed*

to be Hank's standard question.

Judy said, "The answer is that you get those things down—pronto." She turned her back to him, her shoulders shaking from pent-up laughter.

The sight of her made Sonya begin to laugh, too. Even Brad joined in like she hadn't heard him laugh in ages.

Audra cried out between chuckles, "Yeah, but before you take them down, I say this is a perfect opportunity for a snapshot." She ran inside and returned immediately with her camera. "Okay, everybody in front."

Fletcher put out his hand. "May I?"

"Thanks, Fletcher."

As they posed, Judy said, through her teeth, "Audra, I think this group may be gaining position in rank for the strangest group I've ever taken."

"That's the plan," Hank said as Fletcher clicked the camera.

After several poses, Audra promised to send everyone an enlargement. Hank climbed on the cottage roof and began lowering the bikes, assembly-line style.

⁂

A hot breakfast waited: omelets oozing with cheddar, cantaloupe cubes in the perfect shade of orange, and flaky biscuits. Between bites of eggs, it occurred to Sonya that Brad might not be ready to bike again. She asked, "How is your leg?"

He slathered raspberry jam on a biscuit. "Great. . .I think."

"Can I see?"

"I looked. It's a lot better."

Sonya took a sip of juice. "Judy says this is the longest day. Sixty-five miles. Do you think you can make it?"

"We'll find out, won't we?"

"Yeah. I mean, if you overdo it today, you might not be able to finish the trip. I don't want that to happen. You have looked forward to this for so long."

"You're right," he said.

"You don't have to prove anything. Will you stop if it hurts too badly?"

"I'm a big boy. I'll be fine." Brad's neck was turning red, and a vein popped out like a thermometer that had reached its mercury limit.

Sonya looked down the table, and her eyes met with Audra's. *Did she hear them?* Sonya immediately turned back to her plate and absently took a bite of whatever food was closest to her fork.

Fletcher clinked on his water glass with a spoon. "Listen," he boomed.

"Thanks, Fletcher." Judy pushed her plate forward, and the hostess swept in and took it away. In its place, Judy spread a map. "We're in Marthasville. Our destination is Jefferson City, sixty-five miles away. Of course, Fletcher will be your chauffeur if you don't feel like doing the whole trip, for whatever reason. We'll stop at the trailhead, and Fletcher will take us all into the city to our hotel."

Hank whined, "No Killer Hills today?"

"No. Just a killer distance. You'll discover a whole new meaning to the term 'Happy Wagon' after you reach north Jeff City. Trust me."

Sonya watched a cantaloupe cube skid across the table top just short of Brad's lap. Everyone quickly looked at Hank.

Brad picked up the cube and smiled. He said, "You better be careful, bud," and Hank shook in faux horror.

Sonya shook her head. There was no mistaking it; the two had a friend-thing going on. When did that transpire?

"An—ny—way," Judy drew out the word to regain their attention. "We have a long day ahead, so let's not waste any time. Stack your luggage by the trailer, and we'll take off in ten minutes."

Everyone began moving, except Sonya. A long day. Could be good. Could be bad. As Brad said, time will tell. Her thoughts turned to God. *But, Lord, You transcend time. You transcend common sense. I'm glad, because sometimes I feel as if Brad and I are doomed to be stuck in this stagnant marriage unless a miracle comes our way. Could it? Today?*

thirteen

The draft from descending Killer Hill rippled Brad's jacket like a flag in a hurricane. He stopped when he reached the bottom and looked up to see Sonya speeding down, hunched over her bike as she frantically pumped the brakes.

She overshot her stop and made a U-turn back to him. "I don't know which was worse, going up or coming down," she said when she reached him. She wiped tear lines that streaked from the corners of her eyes. Brad realized, for the first time, that she had worn no makeup the last couple of days. The past problems couldn't disguise it: *She's a natural beauty, my wife.*

They followed the streets to the trailhead where the rising sun glowed a fiery orange. Judy waved the bikers to her side. "Since we have such a long ride today, we are going to make good time while it's the coolest—and we're the freshest. From here to McKittrick, we'll form a draft line. Stay single file, don't get so close you overlap tires, and let the head biker set the pace."

"Can I lead?" Hank asked.

"We'll take turns. The leader absorbs the headwinds, so after about ten miles, he or she drops to the end."

Brad fell in single file between Amir and Sonya. The only sounds coming from the group were those of crackling gravel and chains that clinked as gears shifted. Quiet. Coveted quiet.

Without the usual blare of the television, the barrage of clients, or even the silent words of books, Brad's mind was surprisingly without direction. Thoughts and images swirled in and out without rhyme or reason. He wanted to grab hold of one of them and think on it alone, but the idea of committing to a single thought sent fear through his soul. What was going on? Wasn't this opportunity what he had longed for all of these months?

He thought of Sonya pedaling in the middle of the draft line. People surrounded her, but Brad sensed that she felt alone. *Brain, please let another thought flutter in.*

But the other thoughts withdrew. Only Sonya's lonely image stuck.

Stop, brain. This is not what is supposed to happen.

Brad decided to distract himself by fixing his gaze on Amir. For at least fifteen seconds, his mind cleared as he traced the contours of Amir's water pouch. That reminded him of Sonya's hasty bike bag whim. And her habit of impulsive spending. And—

Ugh! God, we need to talk. Brad's vision blurred. *Yesterday was such a disappointment. I trusted that You would help Sonya and me patch things up, but it seems as if we broke apart more. Am I asking the wrong thing? Am I not trying hard enough?* His words seemed to be bouncing off the sky.

Sonya's call broke in. "Brad, Judy says Hank should drop back now. It's your turn to lead."

"Okay. Wish me luck." *I love her, God. That's all I know to say right now. Help me live like I love her.* That peace he coveted. . . it started to come.

&

Brad pulled out to the left and forced his legs to spin at top speed. He passed Amir and reached Hank's side. Brad hollered, "Time's up, buddy! You get to take the tail end!"

"You want to be the big man now, huh?" Hank hollered back.

"Yes, especially if it means I don't have to look at you anymore." Brad laughed. He had never related to many like Hank before. He'd always assumed guys like him were flakes. They were the ones in high school who tied the gym lockers together with tube socks and risked calling the teachers by their first names. Brad had never seen much humor in their thoughtless acts. But now that he was forced to spend time with one of them, he could see a generosity he'd never noticed before. A desire in Hank to gift those around him with smiles and laughter. He looked forward to more time together.

Once in the lead, Brad's focus took a turn. He constantly monitored his speed, and his muscles rebuked him for volunteering to be a draft leader. A slight twinge in his hurt leg traveled to his head in the form of anxiety, but so far, so good.

The Happy Wagon waited at McKittrick. Fletcher was already guzzling root beer. He shook the remaining caramel-colored drops from the can, crushed it, and tossed it. Without a word, he went behind the trailer and jiggled the lock. He bellowed, "Water," like a human bullhorn.

Brad grabbed Sonya's water bottle. "May I?"

She smiled. "Thank you."

"Will you join me?"

"An honor." She laughed. She draped her arm in his, and they rounded the trailer. Plums and oranges filled a cooler next to the water. Even after their big breakfast, the group made a noticeable dent in the food offerings.

Once reassembled, the group listened to Judy's lead. "Eight more miles in the draft line, and then we can pair up again and chat along the way."

Audra put her hand on Sonya's shoulder as they talked. Brad walked over, feeling intrusive, and he asked, "Sonya, will you be the other half of my pair?"

She put her hand on his shoulder and knit her brow sympathetically. "Later, Brad. Audra and I are going to get to know each other better."

For once, he was prepared to listen to her overflow of words, and she didn't care to give him a single drop.

fourteen

At Rhineland, the draft line gave way like an accordion, and Sonya took her place next to Audra. Brad and Hank took the lead, with Amir and Judy in the rear.

Watching Brad pedal ahead made Sonya's heart feel heavy. Not helpful when she needed all of its power to pump blood to her constantly contracting muscles. The heaviness came from a nagging guilt; she, not Hank, should be next to her husband. Especially after he took the effort to ask.

And that guilt didn't stop there. Sonya regretted her unleashed mothering about his leg—a habit that started the day with another emotional wedge between them.

Fortunately, Audra wasted no time before she began asking questions. "So how long have you been biking?"

"Me?" Sonya laughed. "I don't even own a bike. I borrowed Brad's to get ready for this trip."

"Really? I would have tagged you as a long-standing biker." Audra swerved to avoid a tiny black snake that zigzagged across the path. "Amir and I have a quaint, old neighborhood. We bike as often as the sun goes down."

The women continued to exchange trivialities for a few miles. The bluffs at their right seemed to have gotten extra watering from God as they grew higher and higher. The spectacular crags and forms provided an abstract art exhibit, a feast for the eyes and the soul.

"The bluffs leave a bittersweet impression," Sonya said almost reverently. "They are so lovely, so majestic. But also so hard and cold. You can't see past them. Maybe something even more beautiful waits on the other side." She imagined it. "Speckled fawns lapping at pools of water. Golden trees full of chirping birds. . . Life."

They pedaled, listening carefully for more tales from the rock walls. Audra said, "Like us, I imagine. What's hiding behind our walls?"

"Excuse me? I don't understand," Sonya said, but she did. A lump formed in her throat. Audra said nothing. Did she see through Sonya's hesitancy?

Sonya suddenly felt exhausted. Not just her legs but her whole body. "Audra, I—" she began. "I don't know you well, but if I share some things, will you promise not to judge me too harshly?"

"Promise, friend."

"My 'rock walls' are impulsive eating, impulsive shopping. I use them to block out and delay facing the things that hurt. But that just pushes my loving qualities even deeper down, too." The words flowed more easily now. "God is helping me gain control. By giving Him control. Lately, when I feel upset, I talk to Him about it all. And I don't feel as hungry. I don't need more 'stuff.' It's a process."

"Keep with it," Audra said gently. "I see such a lovely heart in you."

"Only because of Christ. Otherwise, I would be a mess!" Sonya smiled. "Well, a *bigger* mess." Somehow, she knew that God had ordained her conversation with Audra. This idea of surrender, now that she voiced it, could be key to more joy in her life. . .and her marriage.

"Stop! Stop up there!" It was Judy's voice from far off.

The four skidded to a halt and headed back until they reached their guide who said, "The recipient of our first flat of the trip goes to Amir."

Sonya's lungs emptied like the tire, relieved that no one reenacted Brad's incident of yesterday.

"Doin' wheelies?" laughed Hank.

"Not exactly," Amir said politely. "Audra, could you get the kit?"

Audra laid her bike in the grass and went to Amir's side. She unzipped his bag and pulled out a neatly organized fix-a-flat kit and a spare tube.

Judy asked, "Do you need any help? Free tube changes are included in the price."

"Thanks, Judy," Amir said. "But we've done this many times, and I think we can manage."

Amir put his hand out, and Audra handed him a rim bar as a surgeon's assistant would a scalpel. He pulled the old tube off, and she folded it neatly into his pack.

"The new tube," Amir requested. She handed it to him, and he kissed her hand. "Ready?"

"Yes." Together, they slid it back on the rim, replacing the tire in fluid motions.

When the couple finished the task, Amir took Audra in his arms and kissed her on the nose. "Thank you, sweetheart. Want to ride together?"

Audra turned to Sonya. "Do you mind?"

She smiled. "Not at all." She met eyes with Brad, who grinned. "Can I take you up on that old offer, hubby?"

"My honor," he said, and they fell in line again, side by side.

Sonya wanted to share her conversation with Audra, but the timing didn't feel right. She opened her mouth, not knowing what she'd say, but Brad beat her to the floor.

"I *am* too serious," he said.

She closed her mouth and blinked a few times.

"You were right. I see it now. Hank, of all people, has liberated me from the chains of irritability. Last night, when I went for a walk. . ." He lowered his voice and relayed a story that made Sonya's hand go over her mouth.

"I can't believe it! You nut!" She squealed. She grabbed her water bottle from its holder, aimed and squeezed hard. A stream of water hit Brad's arm. Instead of his expected scowl, he recanted, shooting her in the leg with his bottle.

"Don't you dare tell," he said, melodramatically, and aimed the bottle at her again. "I have a lot of experience using these."

"Okay," she replied with a stoic face, then, with perfect aim, squirted his nose.

a

At 1:30, the tired, famished group finally reached civilization. The smoky smells from Portland's Riverside Grill wafted from its kitchen outtake vents. The plums eaten at McKittrick had burned as bike fuel miles back.

They sat at the counter, watching the food sizzle in slow motion on the grill. "I am starving," she said to Brad. "I hope you're not embarrassed by how much I am going to gulp down."

"Embarrassed?" Brad swept his hand from her face to her toes. "Look at you. What a gorgeous woman. I'm never embarrassed to be seen with you!"

"What about when I was fat?"

"When?"

"Before I started training for this ride. I've lost fifteen pounds since then."

Brad slapped himself on the head. "*That's* what's different. I knew it wasn't your hair."

"What?" asked Sonya.

"Good for you, honey. I didn't realize. . .till now. Now it's as clear as day."

Sonya squinted at him. The waitress delivered their meals, but neither of them broke their stare.

As an afterthought, Brad chuckled. "You were never fat, honey. And no matter, I'll always think you are the most beautiful woman in the world. Even when you have more wrinkles than I have hair. . ."

Brad took Sonya's hand, and she felt the warmth of his skin meet hers. It seemed to course through her veins, to fill her with happiness. "Let's clean these plates, biker pro."

They both laughed loud enough to make heads turn. Sonya lifted the burger with her free hand, and proclaimed, "Okay. Here goes!" And then, she took a bite.

It tasted like freedom.

a

When only crumbs remained, Judy gave the next round of

directions. They sounded more like a pep talk. "Thirty-five miles down, thirty to go. You can do it, folks. Stay strong."

One more mile sounded like torture to Sonya, but she convinced herself she would make it. She wanted to ask Brad about his leg, but. . .

"Be my partner, gorgeous?" Brad asked, extending his hand.

"Love to."

The first three miles to Mokane felt longer than the first thirty-five. The fatigue spread from their twelve legs to their six heads; even Sonya didn't have much to say. Judy led now, singing in rhythm to her pedals. Sonya cried, "Judy! My friend sang that in church last month."

Sonya never claimed to be a diva, let alone to carry a tune, but she raised her voice to join with Judy's. And when they came to the part that said *His love will meet your every need; seek and you will find it's true,* her voice cracked. But she kept singing.

Brad's eyes seemed glassy, too. But he said nothing.

The song carried them all the way to Mokane. Eight effortless miles. When they found Fletcher holding his usual can of root beer, he ordered them to *Sit!* And he brought them grain bars to eat as they sank into their spots on the ground.

Audra left Amir's side and plopped down next to Sonya. "Thanks for the music."

"Ha!" Sonya said. "If you can call it that."

"No, really. You opened up today. I have issues, too, you know. I tend to rely on my therapist's suggestions. Doc has a lot of wisdom, you know. I try to find the strength within myself to live a good life. But I know there is Someone greater than myself. But I'm not sure who, anymore. And the walls of self reliance I build couldn't block out the truths of your words and that song."

"I'm glad," Sonya said, and she leaned over to hug her new friend.

fifteen

The extended break and warm clothes gave Brad a burst of strength for the last twelve miles. Sonya, on the other hand, began to grow pale, her eyes dull.

"Talk to me," Brad said, concerned. "Tell me about your latest find at the mall."

She shook her lowered head.

"Sing me a song."

"I can't think of any words."

"Okay, then I'll have to." Brad cleared his throat and sang one of Maggie's favorite tunes in falsetto.

Sonya's mouth turned up in a small smile, and a weak laugh escaped.

"Hey, looky there!" Hank called, pointing.

"That's our stop. The capitol building," yelled Judy.

"We're almost there, Sonya," Brad said, spotting the dome in the distance.

"Almost there," she repeated.

Finally, the sight of a man drinking root beer against a blue van soothed their tired eyes. Fletcher slid open the door and commanded, "Get in." No one argued. Single-handedly, the former football player wheeled the six bikes into the trailer.

Once the van got under way, everyone leaned back and closed their eyes. That is, everyone but Hank, who read Jefferson City facts to a captive but disinterested audience. "Did you know that Jefferson City is the only U.S. capital that isn't on an interstate? And no other capital has more letters in its name. And. . ."

At the Plaza Five Hotel, Brad held Sonya against his shoulder as they took the elevator to their room. That night, he didn't even mind letting a bellboy take their luggage up, and he gave him a generous tip out of their few remaining dollars.

The group agreed on a late dinner to allow time for showers and rest. Sonya collapsed on the bed while Brad let steamy water and gobs of lather invade every pore. Then he joined Sonya on the bed.

An hour later, a loud knock woke the unconscious couple. "Dinner!" announced a bass voice.

"Okay, Fletcher. Coming." Brad rubbed his palm over Sonya's back until her eyes stayed open, and they walked to the elevator with the posture of a couple three times their ages.

Back in the elevator, Sonya looked at Brad with heavy eyes. "I did it," she said. "Can you believe I did it?"

You can say it a million times tonight, and I won't care. He smiled with all the energy he could muster. "Yes, honey. I was there."

ðð

The evening's dining took place in a restaurant with barrel tables and vintage farm machinery as décor. But the place also aired romance with checkered tablecloths, high-backed booths, and hurricane lamps at every table.

Dinner hour long gone, the room provided private dining for the bikers, with the exception of an elderly couple huddled away at a corner table. Sonya scooted in a booth next to Brad.

Surprisingly, Amir started the night's conversation. "Sonya," he said, "My wife has had the pleasure of getting to know you, but I haven't. I was wondering, are you a career gal, or do you work within the walls of your home?"

Sonya stared at the man for a moment, then said, "Well, that's a nice way of putting it."

Amir said, "Excuse me?"

"Work within the walls of the home. I like that. That's what I do." Sonya thumped the mustard bottle and drew a golden spiral on her bun. "I used to be a radio talk show host, believe it or not. I never interviewed anyone like Barbra Streisand, but every person I talked to was important, even if they just ran an upcoming blood drive." She took a bite of her sandwich and smiled to herself.

Amir raised his eyebrows. "So that's why you have such a passion for current events. Sonya, I can see you there right now—a lovely girl like you interviewing guests with grace and poise. If you ever do it again, I have several contacts who are, as *you* say, not ranking with Barbra Streisand, but all of us around this table would recognize their names."

"Really?" She got tingles, but her devotion to Maggie overpowered them. "If I went back it would be awhile. I have a pretty important job right now."

Amir took a sip of coffee and smiled. "That's a strong value we share. It's refreshing to see Americans so family oriented. Just remember my offer for the future."

Brad put his fork, tines down, on the corner of his plate. "Excuse me," he said. "I'll be back in a moment."

Sonya patted him on the hand, but he could tell she was still fully engaged in the conversation with Amir.

Brad stumbled back a step and headed to the gift shop at the store entrance. He looked for a trinket to buy little Maggie, but his focus kept wandering back into the dining room.

Thanks to Amir, Brad saw Sonya through the eyes of another admiring man, and he couldn't take his thoughts from her. In addition to her beauty, she had a newfound grace and poise—and competence—he hadn't seen in years.

sixteen

While Brad was gone, Sonya continued describing some unique interviewees she'd crossed on the news show. Amir and Audra seemed impressed, but the suave couple was always polite.

After Brad came back, Audra turned the invisible microphone over to him. "Brad, we haven't heard what you do for a living. You say you work in a gym?"

Brad's mouth was full of baked potato, but he swallowed and said, "Well, I'm a manager for Area Gym in Springfield." Was it Sonya's imagination, or was he turning red? "I run the front desk. Sign up new members. Refer clients to personal trainers. Stuff like that."

"And I can see that you spend some time using the facility, too."

Brad looked at one of his biceps as if he hadn't ever known it was attached to his arm. "Um. . .yes. I work out occasionally."

"Every day," Sonya interrupted, lacing her hands around his upper arm.

"Good for you," Audra said. "It really pays off, doesn't it?"

Brad said, "*I* think so. Now Sonya—"

"Thinks so, too," she interrupted. She thought, *I know what he was going to say. Sonya gripes that I'm there too much.*

"Do you like your job?" Audra asked.

"I've sweated to get to the position for years. I mean work sweat, not exercise sweat."

"It sounds like one worth waiting for."

Actually, Brad was one worth waiting for.

Sonya knew that Audra had no romantic attraction to Brad, but her platonic interest made Sonya take a second look at him.

Sonya realized that the apparent sloth in the brown corduroy chair had always truly been Brad, her successful husband. He

90

was one who had enough motivation to work up to a management position at his job, outselling all of the previous member consultants. All this, without a college degree. Brad hadn't mentioned his level of schooling to Audra; he tried not to let on to anyone. But Sonya knew. He'd worked hard and beat the odds. His secret embarrassment had become her pride today.

Brad took care of his clients, and Brad took care of himself. He was even more attractive than the afternoon Sonya met him at the side of the pool. Not like many men—men who got married, dined on fried everything, and wore their goods under their skin like a ski belt.

But don't forget the best part.

Brad was successful. Brad was fit. But Brad was also redeemed. He found God and walked in His way. Had it not been for that, he would have told Sonya to scram when she signed up for the trip and would have stuck by his guns without remorse. He probably would have told her to scram years ago when the conflicts started.

Sonya sometimes forgot that part. It was easy to do when she let life's problems cause her to forget that God was anywhere.

Sonya slid Brad's fork out of his hand and laced her fingers in its place. "I forgot how proud I was of you," she whispered.

His face looked puzzled. "Didn't I just say that to you?"

"No."

He gave her a little squeeze. "Well, if I didn't, I was sure thinking it."

❧

Brad and Sonya's bike helmets looked out of place thrown in the corner of their Plaza Five hotel room. The couple left their dusty clothes in heaps on the floor and fell into their coveted bed.

"Just think," Sonya mumbled, "No wake up calls. We're only going ten miles tomorrow; we can sleep as late as we want. Or when Fletcher knocks, whichever comes first."

Sonya rolled on her side, and Brad cuddled up close. Her

body felt so heavy that she contemplated leaving the light on. Just as Sonya clicked off the wall lamp, a knock sounded from the door. She pulled her pillow over her ears. Brad called, "Who's there?"

"Hank."

"Hold on." She saw Brad slip on sweat pants and open the door. The stream of light from the hall gave Sonya an instant headache.

"Hey Brad, what's up?"

Now it was Sonya's turn to wish Hank away.

"Not much. Did you see that gift shop at the restaurant? Their inventory hasn't changed since the fifties. . ." Brad's words faded into a faint buzz that took Sonya into an unconscious state. But not for long.

"Oh. Haaaa!" Hank's laugh was an early alarm that yanked Sonya out of her sleep. She felt anger stir. But she was too dreamy to express it. Her muscles screamed from head to toe, *Sleep, Sonya, sleep. Take us out of our misery.*

Hank continued, "And when I found out that. . ." The tingle that preceded sleep filled her brain again, and she welcomed it. For at least a few slow breaths, she retreated from the hotel bed to a world of dreams. Until—

"Hank! You are unbelievable! Then what did you do?"

"I gave it a banana!"

That was the bottom line. Bananas were not topics that merited stealing much needed sleep. She propped herself up on her elbows and called faintly, "Brad? You coming to bed?"

"One second."

"Good. I'm exhausted."

Whispering continued, and suddenly the two burst out laughing. Sonya sat up all the way and rubbed her head. "Brad!" she yelled. "I am not asking you to come to bed, I am *telling* you. Now you tell Hank to take his bananas and jump in an ape pit!"

"Sonya!" Hank exclaimed, and then he laughed even harder. Then she heard Brad's whisper. "Sorry. She's tired, I guess."

"No need to guess about that, husband," Sonya said, unashamed at her eavesdropping.

"Tomorrow, bud," Hank said. Brad shut away the blinding hall light and crawled in bed.

Mr. Double Standard deserved a piece of Sonya's tired mind. "Hey, Mister-I-just-want-to-read-this-Norman-Rockwell-book-and-would-you-leave-us-alone. . .you tell him *I'm* edgy!"

"At least I didn't tell him to jump in an ape pit. We were just about to wind up the conversation, if you'd been patient," Brad said.

"I'm out of patience!"

Brad fell silent. Eventually, he spoke. Softly. Gently. "Of course, Sonya. We biked sixty miles today. I wasn't thinking." He smoothed her hair.

She lay there with her eyes closed but feeling wide open. Her muscles nagged her, which only made matters worse. And a cloud of bitter energy seemed to radiate around Brad, though she knew it came from her, not him.

Dear God, she began. *I'm sorry I was so harsh with Brad. Forgive me. I'm just tired. . .so, so tired. I know You promise a new day tomorrow, but please, don't let it come until it has to. And in the meantime, give me a good. . .a good night's. . .*

જે

Rest. Ah! The sun peeked between the heavy hotel drapes, and Sonya listened to the creaks of people walking in the room overhead. Her muscles whined a bit, but at least they no longer screamed.

The mirror on the dresser's top gave a flip-flop image of the couple on the sag-free bed. Only a tuft of Brad's hair stuck out from the bedspread, and he breathed noticeably from the depth of his lungs. Sonya rolled the covers away from his head. Smiling, she stroked his cheek.

"I'm sorry about last night, Brad."

"Last night?" He scratched his eyebrow. "Oh, yeah." He paused, as if he contemplated saying his next words. "It's okay.

At least now you know how I feel when *you* do that."

Sonya pulled her hand away. "When I do *what*?"

"Nothing," Brad said. "Nothing." He laced his fingers through hers. "How about a prayer to start the day?"

Sonya softened. "Yes, a prayer."

Brad started, but soon they talked to God conversationally, their words flowing as if they were one person uninterrupted by another. Hopes, longings, souls in synch.

Unexpectedly, Brad pulled her arm closer until they held each other face to face. Sonya melted as he kissed her on both eyes, her nose, and then her mouth.

A knock interrupted the moment. Sonya said under her breath, "If that's Hank, he's not going to be able to pedal a mere ten miles after I get done with him."

Brad laughed and kissed her again. Another knock.

"Mornin'!"

"Morning, Fletcher!" Brad yelled back. He pecked Sonya on the head, and she giggled.

"Breakfast!" Fletcher announced.

Brad and Sonya's eyes met, and Sonya shook her head.

"No thanks," called Brad. "You can have ours."

seventeen

"How's your leg today?"

Finally, Brad could lay that question to rest for good. "With the exception of an ugly mark, I wouldn't know I'd wiped out. Now my aching hamstrings—they're another story."

The two stepped on the elevator. Sonya said, "Tell me about it! If I was a guitar, I'd say someone got a little enthusiastic tuning me. My muscles are so tight, they could pop any minute."

Though Brad hardly wished pain on his wife, he felt relief to hear that her muscles shared the same repercussions as his. In retrospect, he wished he'd taken her up on offers to train for the trip. But she had asked him ten times a day, and he turned her down, a stubborn mule.

The enclosed elevator amplified the growl that came from Sonya's stomach. She looked up sheepishly and said, "Don't get me wrong. . .I'm glad we missed breakfast, but my stomach is not too happy about it."

Brad unzipped the duffel bag and pulled out two protein bars: one peanut, one banana. "Take your choice."

Sonya braced herself against the wall as she suddenly shook with laughter. "If you think I would even consider banana, you need to think again!"

"Oh, I forgot."

She took the peanut butter.

Sonya's smile faded, and she said, "Well, I didn't forget. Brad, I am terribly sorry about last night. I wasn't thinking straight. Forgive me."

He put his arm around her and pulled her close. "That was a done deal already."

"Brad, I—" Sonya's sentence stopped in midair, and her face

resembled a scared deer. The elevator door had opened, and the group waited in the lobby, staring at them with dumb smiles.

Audra's camera flashed. She said, "I'll order an enlargement."

&

As Brad filled his water bottle at the trailhead, he noticed that Hank stayed in the van. Brad peeked in. "Wimping out today?"

Hank hopped out. "Didn't you notice?" He held out beet-colored hands that matched his painfully red face.

Brad gritted his teeth. "Ouch. A sunburn in October?"

"I could get a sunburn at night if I stayed out long enough."

Brad patted his back. "Sorry, bud."

Hank recoiled. "Hey, watch it!"

&

In the parking lot, Amir checked the air in his tires. He stuffed the gauge in his pack and looked at Brad. "I'd enjoy riding with you today, Brad."

Brad looked at his wife. "Sonya?"

She smiled and nodded, winking.

The chalk-covered bikes seemed old friends that morning. But after Brad sat on his, he wondered if "old enemy" was a more suitable title.

Minus Hank, they crossed a bridge to start the trip. The tiny bounces over every slat made Brad wish for a sunburn excuse, too. He was relieved when, only a mile later, Judy stopped the group and made them do ten minutes of stretches.

"I've always encouraged my clients to stretch, but I'm bound to be fanatical about it from now on," Brad said to Amir.

Amir reached for his ankle. "Yes, freeing up that lactic acid does wonders."

"I'm impressed—you know fitness jargon."

"I didn't go to an Ivy League school for nothing."

"Where?" Brad said, impressed again.

"Somewhere in the east, you know. It was a long time ago." Whatever school it was, they must have had Humility 101 among the general core classes.

The five started down the trail again. . .another day of the sun's rays to paint warm streaks on the autumn leaves. Today there was an added bonus of the Missouri River flowing yards from the trail with bright sparkles bouncing off its dull, muddy waters.

The two pedaled in silence until Judy and Sonya started up with another duet. Sonya sang soprano, Judy alto. Their voices flowed with the river's currents and the rhythm of their legs. Brad wished to close his eyes to absorb every nuance of the sounds.

When the ladies started on a peppier tune, Amir asked Brad, "What kind of music do you like?"

"Depends on my mood."

"Flexible, huh?"

"Or picky. Depends on how you look at it. How about you?"

Amir smiled. "I enjoy jazz kings like Louie Armstrong. But I also love classical piano."

"Yeah, I've played a lot of that stuff."

Amir raised an eyebrow. "Really?"

"Years ago." Somehow Brad's answer didn't sound humble.

"Why did you stop?"

Brad's silence said volumes.

Amir stuck his water pack straw in his mouth. His Adam's apple dipped a few times before he dropped the thin tube again.

Brad hesitated, then prayed. *You know, I've fooled myself into thinking I had moved on from the disappointments of the past. But all I've done is push them down deeper. You drive a hard bargain, God. Truth for freedom. But I'm ready to reveal the truth to move on.*

He sensed inaudible words: *The truth will set you free.*

Even through his sweat pants, Brad could see the thick muscles in his legs contract. They were a prize for good work, new resolutions, and abandoned talents. Before Brad changed his mind, he began, "We had a piano in our house. Piano lessons were my parents' big splurge. I took them every week, and I practiced every day. To be honest, I got pretty good at it. We had a talent show at my junior high one evening, and while most of the kids did dances to disco or goofy skits, I played Beethoven. My performance was almost flawless, but one of the popular kids made a crack as I bowed. His crowd used my talent as bait to taunt me in the halls."

Amir clicked his tongue. "That is tragic. How awful."

"I wanted things to be different. A good friend invited me to his church, and I found a new strength. When the kids poked fun, I had an advocate by my side. They didn't get to me anymore. Well, not as much, anyway. Still, it seemed like a new start, so I threw out the piano books and got a job and a gym membership. And it was like a purging of the old self, a re-creation of Brad Kane. A few years later, I met Sonya. She didn't know weak Brad—just the Brad *you* know now. So I've always thought, why change a good thing?"

"Where good exists, there is potential for better."

Brad tuned out the trail noises. *Better?* Could re-embracing parts of the past allow an improvement for the days of the future? He'd been more of a problem solver in the past. But maybe it was time to go a step further. To find ways to grow, not just ways to keep from being broken.

Amir smiled. "I'm glad you shared. Maybe your God has a way of piecing your childhood back together into a stronger whole."

"Like muscles?" Brad asked.

Amir nodded. They both knew that when muscles are exerted, the stress breaks their fibers, and after they heal they grow back even stronger. The concept is central to strength training. *Is that how God builds one's spirit—through exertion and brokenness?*

Brad looked up. *If it's so, Lord, then let me be broken.*

❧

Hartsburg's annual Pumpkin Festival was in full swing as the bikers paraded into town. In fact, the town had its own parade, featuring a Pumpkin King who tossed wrapped candy to open-mouthed children who held out their hands along the streets.

Judy talked loudly over the crowd's roar, "Guys, you will bed down at the Skye Bed-and-Breakfast. Gals will stay at the Daisy Cottage."

Brad wondered if anyone would object to the arrangement, but Audra and Sonya had already laced arms and started chattering nose to nose, clearly showing that a night of separation from their husbands wouldn't traumatize them.

And yet, Brad had mixed feelings. On one hand, the thought of sacking out with a bunch of guys who didn't take thirty minutes to get ready for bed brought a hint of a smile to his face. And yet Sonya was still his preferred roommate. By far.

The Happy Wagon drove off with the giggling girls. Silent, the men simply grabbed their scanty possessions and tromped up the porch steps. Brad kept his eye on the navy van that traveled southbound, causing him to trip over a tabby cat on the wood-planked porch.

The owner, Crawford, a stately man with graying temples, parted the screen door barrier. He welcomed them with a smile that made the wrinkles around his watery, sky blue eyes smile, too. "Let me show you to your rooms."

The hotel had been booked months in advance for the Pumpkin Festival. As a result, the men had two rooms between them. Randomly paired, Brad and Hank were shown to the room they would share. Its space reflected the décor of an 1890s hotel. Less capricious than their first bed-and-breakfast, but still nice. Clean and simple with wood floors, tall wardrobes, and room sinks stocked with miniature toiletries in wicker baskets. The guests shared a common bathroom with a stand-up shower. Amir got first dibs.

Brad and Hank decided to unpack. "I like this place," Hank said, examining the room as if he was a prospective buyer. He sprayed the faucet until it steamed and opened all of the dresser drawers and wardrobe doors. "Look at these!" he said, reaching in the wardrobe and holding out two thick, white robes by their collars. He threw one at Brad. "Try it on."

Brad tossed it back at him. "No thanks."

"Your loss," Hank chirped, and he pulled his clothes off into knotted balls and strapped the robe around his body. Sitting in a corner chair, he folded his arms and sighed. "This is the life." The sleeves hung to his knuckles, and the hem was ballroom length on his short frame.

"You look like one of the Seven Dwarfs," Brad said with a smirk.

Hank stood and flopped a handless sleeve at his roommate. "Hi ho, Grumpy!"

The shower stopped running, and Amir emerged in a robe that was sibling to the two Hank had found. He held a hardcover book in his hand, but stopped at Brad's door. Smiling, he said, "I feel newly inspired. You can't beat coming out from a near-scalding shower with nothing to do but relax. Normally, I'm off and running before my hair has time to dry. Not today. I'm going to lock myself in and do some reading." He held up the book and tapped it. And he went in his room and shut the door.

"My turn," Brad sang.

Hank tried to beat him to the bathroom door, but Brad's sweat pants provided better aerodynamics than Hank's terrycloth robe.

Two showers later, the men wore clean skin and clean clothes. Brad sat in the corner chair, absorbed in the moment.

"You wanna check out the festival?" Hank asked, antsy.

"Lead the way!" Brad answered and wondered if the girls had the same idea. Hopefully.

eighteen

Everything about the Daisy Cottage said feminine: lace curtains, hanging quilts, china teacups. Sonya dropped her duffel bag and wandered around the living room as if in a museum. Tasseled antique lamps glowed dimly, and handcrafted work sprawled through the rich wood. She ran her fingers over their textures and inhaled their musty smells.

At the top of the stairway, the women's rooms waited with thick comforters and wooden dressers topped with white-glazed pitchers. They all went in one and dropped their luggage. "I'm so glad today was our ten-mile day," Sonya said in a dreamy voice. "I would have hated coming here yesterday when I was delirious with exhaustion."

"Yeah. Now we have two rooms to divvy out between us three," Judy said. "I'll let you choose who stays with whom."

Audra shrugged. "I say we all hang out together, and the last one to surrender to sleep gets the other room all to herself!"

"Brilliant, Audra. All agreed?"

"Aye," said the trio.

$\approx$

The three pulled out scented gels, soaps, and shampoos and pooled them as community property. Sonya grabbed a few bottles, along with a rolled towel. Once in the shower, she caught herself singing praises as she lathered up, massaging soap deep into her hair down to the cracks between her toes. The murky water eddied down the drain, starting to turn clear.

Refreshed in body and soul, Sonya dried and dressed, feeling as pretty as her surroundings. "Next?" she announced, the bedroom's cool air hitting her as she exited.

Audra stepped in.

Judy reclined on the quilt-covered bed. "You're holding up

well," she said, staring at the ceiling. "Not everybody makes it this far without hopping in the van."

"But you, my singing partner, have to take some of the credit," Sonya laughed.

"Oh, but that husband of yours helped you through the hardest stretch when he chimed in."

Sonya sat on the corner of the bed. "You know, you're right. I can hardly remember the last part of the ride. I don't *want* to remember!"

"You two seem close. You care about each other deeply, even when you have your differences."

Sonya stiffened. *Close?* "We haven't been close for a long time, believe it or not. I was hoping this trip would have that effect, though."

"Well, it looks like your plan is working."

Feeling a bit vulnerable, Sonya changed the subject. "What do you make of Hank? I notice how patient you are with him."

Judy chuckled. "That kid has a way of getting under your skin and irritating you in a way that's surprisingly amusing. It's refreshing to be with someone who isn't afraid to live out of the mainstream. As Hank matures, he'll settle down a bit. And if not, his future wife will see to it."

Sonya felt a lump in her throat. She wrestled with an unwelcome thought. *Have I doused the flame that used to make Brad's eyes twinkle?* All she could say was, "How depressing."

"To a point. A little discipline does a man good. He can find matching socks and starts eating foods that don't have additives as their primary ingredient. But when a wife crosses the line into criticism, it can crush her husband's spirit."

"And how do you know where that line is?"

"When you notice what's wrong with him more than what's right."

Ouch.

The bathroom door opened and a squeaky clean Audra emerged. "Ready, Judy?"

Judy scooped up an armful and stepped in.

Audra chirped, "What luxury to walk out of a shower without a kid waiting at the door for something."

"One is hard enough. I admire you, O-Mother-of-Four," Sonya said.

Audra parted her hair with the tail of her comb. "Amir's a gem. He does work long hours, but when he's home, we work as a team."

A team. Hardly a word to describe Brad's and her approach to raising Maggie. Sonya was more like a dentist—pulling teeth to get help. She blew out a breath. "Must be nice."

"Yeah." Audra slid a tortoise shell comb through her long hair. "From your tone of voice, I read that you and Brad aren't always on the same wavelength."

"That keen perception of yours again."

Audra sighed. "I think it's hard being the man."

Sonya laughed. "Are you insane! They have it easy!"

Audra rummaged through her purse. "Well, think of it this way. What if every day you had to show up for the end of Brad's shift, and he handed his work over to you where he left off?"

"I could handle it."

"But he assumes that you can do the job as well as he does—even though he does it all day and you don't show up till its time to tie up loose ends."

"Okay, that would be rough," Sonya admitted. "But a child is not a job. Maggie is a little girl who just needs affection and guidance."

"It's easy for you to feel that way. I can tell Brad feels competent at work, but maybe he lacks that confidence with your Maggie."

Sonya cried, "But she's just a little girl!"

"Have you ever sent Brad on a grocery store run? And he comes home with the wrong flavor of yogurt? Or maybe picante sauce instead of salsa?"

Sonya nodded. "Sugar cereal. He knows Maggie shouldn't eat it. He gets the radioactive-looking stuff in colors God did not design to be ingested."

"You corrected him?"

I even took it back one time. Sonya felt her voice fight to rise again. She took a deep breath and said, "He needed to know."

"I know how it goes. You said something like, 'Next time get the other stuff.' But he heard, 'You did it wrong.' It's how a lot of men's ears are wired to their brains. It's the same with matching Maggie's outfits or reading her the right bedtime story. You believe you know the best way to be Mommy, but you have to let *him* be Daddy his way."

How dare she make such assumptions! But the flare of Sonya's anger extinguished quickly. Audra, the self-proclaimed truth teller lived up to her reputation. *I am the truth.* Could Jesus be speaking through Audra—bringing a healing balm to Sonya's past cuts at Brad? Sonya asked, "Have you and Judy been comparing notes?"

"What?"

"Oh, nothing. You both have such wisdom." Wisdom that Sonya tucked away for Brad's and her return to Springfield life. Wisdom that left her a little scared of possible outcomes. She could see it now. Maggie wearing rags to school, while the refrigerator rack became covered with ginseng tea and not a drop of milk. "But Audra," she objected, "It seems that Brad doesn't want to learn to do things the right way."

"Is there a right way?" Audra asked. " 'Cause if there is, tell me. I'd like to sign up for that course."

"You know what I mean," Sonya said. "You can't live with his dirty socks permanently on the floor."

"Then stuff them in his pillow case. That'll get the message across."

Sonya's mouth dropped open. "Audra! You can't be serious."

She shrugged. "It speaks louder than an hour long lecture, and if handled right, it can be a lot of fun." Audra's smirked, then her face became stoic. "Hey, don't miss my point here, Sonya. Your relationship is more important than dirty socks. If he never threw them in the hamper again, would you leave him over it?"

"Absolutely not!"

"Then tell him what you want, tell him again, stuff the socks in his pillow case, and go on with life even if he never gets it. Okay?"

"Okay." She'd try it.

"Ready for another hard truth?"

"I don't know. But try me." Sonya prayed for humility on the spot.

"Our husbands have issues with us, too. Issues that can make socks look like party favors."

The words hung in the air. Hard words. Freeing words.

I am the truth. The truth will set you free.

Sonya took unexpected joy in knowing it was okay to accept Brad's imperfections.

A few minutes later, Judy reentered the bedroom, dressed and fresh "I'm scoping out the Pumpkin Fest. Anyone else coming?"

❧

The three women walked back out onto the street in outfits that would fall apart like wet tissue paper on a long bike ride: leather boots, form-fitting jeans, embroidered sweaters. They headed toward the sound of organized pandemonium, passing a classy bike shop. "Want to check it out?" Judy asked, pointing at the neon sign.

The roasted scent of coffees mingled with a mellow sweetness. Not only did the shop sell equipment and cycle wear, but they also poured up mocha drinks and cracked open jars of biscotti for those in need of blood-sugar boosts.

Sonya and Audra wandered to the back room where equipment hung in neat rows. Sonya picked up what looked like a couple of bent pipes and turned them over in her hands.

Audra glanced at Sonya through the corner of her eye. She said, "Those are great. Amir swears by them."

"What are they?"

"Bar ends. You clip them on the ends of your handlebars,

and they allow you to reposition your hands and body so you don't get as sore."

"What I wouldn't give for that. I never dreamed that after a day of riding, my hands would be in the top five list for most tired parts of my body." She gripped the bent bars more tightly and moved on.

After flipping through the T-shirts and picking out a blue water bottle, Sonya went to check out. She opened the biscotti jar and chose a pecan-studded cookie.

"Bar ends. . .bottle. . .and biscotti." The cashier punched in the items. "Thirty dollars and five cents."

Sonya slapped her credit card on the table, but a little voice inside said, *A bit of discomfort in the hand may be preferable to another blow to the pocketbook. Brad is right. Your mom has proved it. Spur-of-the moment purchases advertise happiness but rarely deliver.* Swallowing her pride, Sonya slid the bottle and the bike parts to the side of the black-topped counter. "I'm sorry, I changed my mind. Just the cookie, please."

"Okay. Make that seventy-five cents."

She paid cash and savored the biscotti in small bites. Brad's face flashed across Sonya's mind, and she wished she could see him—could tell him about the Daisy Cottage and about her victory over an impulse buy.

The crowd thickened with each step, and smoke ballooned under peppermint-striped canopies just ahead. And the pumpkins. . .

Round, tall, big, small, painted, carved. Sonya had a sudden craving for pumpkin bread.

nineteen

On the festival streets, Hank picked a brown teardrop-shaped object from a box that advertised PIG'S EARS. YOUR DOG WILL LOVE 'EM. "Want one?" he said.

"If I had a tail and barked, maybe I'd consider it," Brad said, his humored tone hanging by a thread. He was getting tired, and for the last half hour , he'd combed the mass of people for a Sonya he never found.

The prospect of hot food drove him on. Funnel cakes, apple butter, and a huge variety of homemade delicacies waited under a tent by the Hartsburg Church. The bakery merchants covered the top of a folding table with hundreds of offerings in plastic wrap. Behind those sat a money box and a shorthaired gal in a lawn chair. The girl had round, aqua eyes and a voice that resembled Maggie's.

"You lived here long?" Hank asked her after she made change with her previous customer.

"All eighteen years of my life," she answered, turning the one-dollar bills so that each George Washington faced the same direction.

"Do you grow pumpkins?"

"No. August Klemme started the crop almost a hundred years ago for hog feed. Now the Sapps and Hackmans are the main pumpkin farmers. They grew a hun'red thousand this year. All kinds. Howden, Baby Pam Pie, Jack Be Little, Field, Connecticut. Even Big Max."

"How about plain old orange?" Hank cried.

The girl just stared at him with a confused expression in those aqua eyes.

"Uh hmm, could I have a muffin please?" Brad said, trying to save his friend.

"Fifty cents, sir. . . . Did ya see the parade?"

Brad looked at Hank as if to say, *You answer.*

Hank nodded. "On the way into town. We're riding across Missouri on the Katy Trail." The girl looked up in interest. Hank pulled a butter creme disk from his pocket. "The Pumpkin King threw this to me. Saved it for you."

"Oh, okay." She took it and put it in the change box with the pennies.

They all stood there, suspended in an awkward pause.

"Why don't we sit down somewhere?" Brad said to Hank.

"Okay," Hank replied. He waved at the girl. "Bye. See ya around."

She held up the candy piece. "Bye. Thanks."

Brad and Hank had not walked ten yards when an unexpected hug almost caused Brad's muffin bite to go down the wrong pipe.

"Hi, Sweetie!"

"Sonya!" Even though she wore a sweater and jeans, she looked elegant. All clean and colorful and strawberry-scented. "Hi, pretty." Brad tapped his chest a few times, then opened his arms for a hug.

After a quick embrace, Sonya pointed to his muffin. "Where did you get that?"

"Over there. Want a bite?"

"I'd say! Not just a bite. One of my own."

"Can I show you the way?" he asked.

She turned to the other women. "Okay?"

"Of course," Judy said.

The couple wove through the crowd toward the canopy. Brad could see Hank crawling under the table to a vacant lawn chair next to the round-eyed young lady. The redhead sat down.

The girl hiccuped her chair over a few inches. Hank did the same and propped his elbows on the table.

Sonya reached for some pumpkin bread. "That'll be fifty cents," the girl recited. She pretended to ignore Hank, though her eyes kept flipping to the right.

Sonya slid over some quarters, peeled away the bread's wrap, and took a bite. Brad cued in on Hank's conversation.

"You've got the best booth by far. Did you make all these delicious muffins?"

The girl giggled. "No. But I helped."

"Well, I'd give you a blue ribbon."

Brad smirked. *Tone it down, buddy. She'll see right through it.*

Sure enough, the girl squinted at him. "I don't remember you buying anything."

"I. . .uh. . ." Hank tried to buy time. "I'll take a dozen." He tilted to the side to pull some money from his jeans pocket.

After Hank had dug out a dollar bill, three nickels, and some ticket stubs that had gone through the wash cycle a few times, a woman with gray-streaked hair came and stood behind Hank. "Hi, son. I think you're in my chair."

"Oh, sorry!" he said, a little too loudly. He hopped up, pulled out the lawn chair, and waved his hand with a flourish. "Be my guest."

The woman rolled her eyes and sat. "Danielle, I hear they're almost out of ribs at the caboose."

"Ribs!" Hank licked his lips.

"Yeah," said young Danielle. "They serve up barbecue in a restored train car. You want me to show you where?"

Hank crawled under the table again and stood next to Brad. He whispered, "You'll forgive me for abandoning you, won't you?"

"Go get 'em," Brad coaxed.

Danielle walked around the table, and the couple disappeared into the crowd.

Brad gave a knowing look to the gray-haired woman who peered suspiciously at Hank. "Ma'am?"

"Hmmm?" She kept her eyes targeted on the back of Hank's head.

"No need to worry about him."

"You had better be right," she answered, finally looking away. She began to reorganize the table display when she came upon the lint-infested pile that Hank had just scraped from his pocket. "This yours?"

"No. But it's yours now."

"Don't want it," she squawked, but she picked out the coins, shook off the dollar bill, and stuck the handful in the money box with the newest George Washington conforming to the others.

Sonya took her last bite and wiped her mouth. "So what have you been up to?"

Brad took her hand, and they began walking. "Wearing white robes, being hungry, learning about Big Max. Not much. How about you?"

Sonya knitted her brow, then smiled. "Fantastic! We checked into the Daisy Cottage, and the place is stunning. You should come over and see the wallpaper; it would look gorgeous in our entryway at home. . .vanilla lotion. . .Audra. . ." Brad's tired mind could not track his wife's words. The crowd's roar made his head hurt, and he wanted to sit down ". . .don't know what the sleeping arrangement will be tonight. . .bought bar ends."

Brad's ears perked up. "You bought what?"

Sonya frowned and released his hand. "Nothing, Brad. Were you listening?"

"You said you bought bar ends." He had been wanting some for months, but the trip consumed too much of their money for the luxury.

"No, I said that I *almost* bought them. But I changed my mind—even after the cashier rang them up. I thought you'd be happy."

Brad crossed his arms. "Yes. Okay."

Sonya's eyes fell on the ground, and her shoulders slouched. *What did I do wrong now?* "Good, Sonya. Where did you say you *almost* bought them?"

"Bike Depot. Two doors up from the Skye."

He patted her on the back. The crowd grew thicker by the minute. A short, heavy woman carrying a painted pumpkin pushed past him. He begged, "Can we sit down somewhere?"

"I was hoping to look for a present for Maggie at a craft booth. Let's scope out the booths before all the good stuff's gone," Sonya persisted.

Brad pointed. "I think I see the girls. Why don't you catch up with them, okay? I'll be fine."

Sonya put her hand on his arm. "Really? Thanks. Get some rest."

Fortunately, Brad's bed-and-breakfast was a pumpkin's throw away. He dragged his feet down the road, up the inn's stairs, and down the hall.

"Hello, Brad. How was the festival?" Amir's door was cracked open enough that Brad could see him reading in a brass bed, a trio of pillows propped behind him.

"Fine," Brad said, not wanting to go into details. He began to push his own door open and paused, peeking at Amir again. "Umm. . .how about you?"

"Wonderful," Amir said, holding up a bottle of iced cappuccino as if performing a toast. "I'm clean, rested, and alone."

Alone? *A hint?* "Sorry to disturb you," Brad said, stepping back toward his door. He related easily with Amir's definition of luxury.

"No. Come in." The dark-skinned man tipped his chin up, emptying the last drops of the nut-brown drink into his mouth.

"What are you reading?"

"*Mere Christianity.* My mind loves a good challenge."

"Is that how you see Christianity? As a mental challenge?"

"In a way. It's intriguing and fresh. I was raised in a Muslim family, and Audra was raised without any particular belief whatsoever. In my home, we didn't really practice religion. I guess we were Americanized—secularized."

A few springs creaked as Brad sat on Fletcher's bed. "What part strikes you most?"

Amir paged through the book. "The man Jesus. So wise, so sensitive. But so. . .so. . .rebellious, almost."

"I never thought of Him exactly that way," Brad said.

"Really? And you claim to know Him?"

"Yes. I *do* know Him. And I strive to be like Him. . . . Now that you mention it, I guess I'm a little rebellious, too. Take work, for example. A gorgeous woman keeps making advances at me, and even though most of the guys see no harm in my being friends with her, I won't. They think I'm nuts. I rebel against the current mind-set, if you put it that way. If I'm prayerful, rebellion from natural, selfish actions seems normal."

"I see that some kinds of rebellion can be productive. It sounds like you know that kind."

"The normal Christian life is abnormal," Brad said. "We're non-conformists." Brad believed it, but he knew he failed to practice it sometimes. "At least I try to be. I'm learning what that means more each day. Even on this trip. Especially in my marriage."

Amir tapped his lip with a finger. "I like the way your religion sounds. Purposeful."

"Yes, purposeful," Brad mirrored. "I just wish I could live it as well as I talk it. Amir, for a nonbeliever, you sure do have a handle on certain aspects of the faith."

"Maybe the sociology of it. Maybe even the practicality, Brad. But I don't know your Jesus."

"That can change," Brad said.

"Yes, maybe so."

Maybe now? Maybe later? What was Amir thinking?

Brad didn't push it. But he did ask another question. "You say your parents didn't place much stock in religion. But what do you want for your children?"

Amir's eyes softened. "More than I can give them. I teach them right. I teach them wrong. But it is not enough. That's more apparent the older my children become."

"Christianity is more than believing the Bible or following rules or traditions. It is about letting Christ share his love through us," Brad said. Between his sentences, he wedged mini-prayers for the right words to come. "Our Maggie has another whole family at our church. Brothers and sisters and grandparents and uncles. They watch out for her, encourage her every week. And because of Jesus, those rights and wrongs have a source. They are not just arbitrary values. They are His ways."

"You are wise, Brad."

"Not really. The foolishness of God is wiser than men. I just have the mind of Christ. At least I try to remember that I do." God heard Brad's prayers. Brad's explanations were reminders—even to his own heart. Rather than murk up their message, he decided to let the words linger in the air. He said, "I'll let you get back to that wonderful aloneness you've been having. I want to get some of that, too."

"Thank you, Brad," Amir said with a peaceful smile.

"My pleasure. If you want to talk more, don't hesitate to knock."

"I'll remember."

Brad wandered back to his empty room, tossed his shoes on the wooden floorboards, and flopped down on the bed. "Father, help Amir feel your touch," he started. But those were the only words he remembered saying before he slipped into an unconscious place void of words.

❧

"Dinner!"

Brad would know that voice anywhere now. He rolled toward the door. "Coming, Fletcher. I'll meet you there."

Hank had not returned. Brad was glad for the uninterrupted nap. He splashed his face with water from the sink and stretched his arms as high as they could reach.

He was the last to arrive at Dorothy's Cafe, not that it mattered. Because of the festival, the waiting list filled two sheets of paper. He told Judy, "I need to do something. I won't be long."

Sonya said, "Where are you going?"

Brad simply looked at his watch and replied, "I'll be back even before they seat us."

And he was. Finally, a waitress led the group to three tables she had shoved together. Another long half-hour later, the tabletop was filled with home-style foods and tall, iced drinks, which all disappeared in a flash. The conversation never died as each person shared tales of his day. Brad knew by the gleam in Hank's eye that he was holding out on Danielle details.

Amazing that after all the food they'd already downed, they consumed two whole pies. The spikes in the bike pedals must have made holes in their feet. Now full, everyone's eyes drooped.

Sonya stood, walked to Brad, and kissed him on the cheek. "Sleep tight, honey. I'm going home."

En masse, the rest of the crew scooted their chairs back and praised the meal with tummy pats and last minute bites of the leftovers. Grabbing toothpicks and mints, they exited. Brad and Hank ventured off in the opposite direction of the girls, over the Skye's porch, and up its brown-painted stairs.

When the two men reached their room, they both flopped down on their beds.

Hank said, "This life-sucking sunburn has wiped me out. It took all of my energy to ignore it when I was with Danielle."

"You sure it wasn't Danielle who had this effect on you?" Brad asked.

Hank put his finger to his lips and looked pensive, as if he'd been asked to explain the theory of relativity. "No," he said. "No, I'm *not* sure."

Brad smirked. "So tell me about this mind-draining phenomenon named Danielle. You've been keeping her a secret all night."

"Danielle, Danielle," Hank sang. "Eyes as blue as sapphires, a laugh that puts the splash of the old Missouri River to shame."

"Sounds like you're quoting from Song of Solomon, twenty-first century style."

"Never heard of him," Hank answered. "Is he a 1960s dude?"

"No, he's a B.C. dude." Brad chuckled.

"I don't read that comic strip either. . . . Anyway, Danielle's nice. And if you don't mind me saying, she's a babe, like your wife."

Brad hadn't thought of Sonya in those terms for many years. She'd been beautiful. Exquisite. But not a *babe*. His housewife/partner in parenting companion had become a "babe" on wheels. He pictured Sonya at the Daisy Cottage, gabbing with the other women, holding their attention with a million bits of trivia and sentiment. And he missed her. Badly.

Hank waved his hand in front of Brad's eyes. "Hey, listen! We got ribs at the train car and ate them off the same plate. Very romantic."

"I can imagine." Sitting in an old train with sticky, orange-colored sauce all over their faces and fingers. One step up from fast food.

Hank pulled a ripped piece of paper out of his pocket. "I got her number."

Brad gave him a supportive thumbs-up.

"Gotta have her number if I'm gonna marry her," Hank said, waving the scrap.

Brad opened his eyes wide. "What! You can't be serious."

"I *did* ask her," Hank said. "But no, I wasn't serious."

"And she knows this?"

Hank jutted his bottom lip out. "Yeah. Even if she did think I was, it wouldn't matter. She whacked me on the head and yelled, 'No way!' I think she knocked half of my freckles off." He shook his head and said, "It's a cold, cold world."

"I'd never have the gall to ask a girl to marry me within hours of meeting her. Even if I *were* joking. You are so confident. So self-assured."

"Me?"

"Yeah. You've brought me out of my shell on this trip."

It was true. How gracious Sonya had been to put up with his moods. But that was changing. . . .

"Me!" Hank yelled. "Ha!" He rolled off the bed and walked to the mirror that hung over the washbowl. He pulled off his shirt, exposing outlines of rows of ribs. Then he flexed his arm, and a mound the size of a tulip bulb popped up. "Look at this massive display of muscle and brawn," he said, turning to face Brad. He grabbed the skin on his bicep between his fingers and pulled it taut. "Just try to top that."

"Your body is not all that matters."

"Yeah, *I* know that. But how many times do you see women fill out a request at a dating service like this: 'Pair me up with a short redheaded guy. Skinny as an alley cat and nutty as a squirrel.'"

"But you're so fun to be around." How strange that Brad gave Hank the pep talk when he thought he was the insecure one.

"What do you know about me, Brad?" Hank asked.

"You eat a lot. You sunburn easily."

"And. . ."

"And you like ribs."

"And. . ."

No answer.

"See?" Hank said. "It's easy to joke all the time. At least it is for me. But you're the confident one. You talk to people—let them know what's going on inside."

"But you risk being laughed at," Brad said. "I say something, and I think, did I say something wrong? What should I have said instead? What are they thinking?"

Hank put his hands on his hips. "Okay. You convinced me. We're both messed up."

"All right!" Brad said, and they high-fived in the air.

Hank sat down on Brad's bed. "In my case, you wonder what any woman would see in you. And then a sweetheart like Danielle comes along and accepts you. Even when you look like a lobster."

"Yeah?"

"Brad, you have no idea what I am talking about. Just look at you. All you have to do is stretch, and all the girls in a hundred mile radius will swoon."

"Hardly!" Brad said, convinced that Hank's compliments were simply insincere attempts to return his. "I could hardly believe my ears when Sonya said 'I do' at our wedding. She was like a dream." *And still is.*

"So there's hope for me, huh?"

"The girl ate ribs with you, didn't she? The most fattening, messy food on earth. Definitely not female cuisine. She's probably telling her friends, 'I gained two inches for that man.' And she wishes you'd called her yesterday."

"Hmm. . . I'll have to remember the rib test," Hank said. "That's almost as sure as an engagement ring."

"I wouldn't go *that* far!" Brad chuckled. He suddenly sat up. "I'm going for a walk." Hank reached for a shoe. "No. By myself. There's something I have to do."

Hank winked and nodded, knowingly.

"Not what you think, Hank. I will admit this has something to do with the bikes, but I'm not pulling any pranks tonight."

twenty

Morning hit. Sonya guessed that she might have felt more refreshed after a night in the van. Her legs demanded to be stretched, and she couldn't imagine what contorted position her aching neck must have assumed. When she opened her eyes, she realized that her feet were where her head should have been. With a yawn, she stretched them in opposite directions on the bed. Clattering sounds met the wood floor as loose checkers rained down from the quilted comforter.

Over Audra's sleeping form, Sonya spotted Judy brushing her teeth in the bathroom. The woman gargled, then realized she was on stage. Dabbing her mouth with a towel, she said, "Morning, Sonya."

"You sleep in the other room?" She couldn't remember.

"No. No one made it. I woke up at the foot of the bed, curled in a ball. Seems we all conked out sometime between crock pot recipes and sunup."

"Ugh! My body aches worse than it did after riding yesterday."

"Nothing a few pancakes and a few miles on the trail can't cure."

Sonya flopped back down. "I hope you're right."

When the women rejoined the men after breakfast, Sonya itched to tell Brad the highlights of her night. She found him on the Skye's porch swing and plopped down beside him.

"Morning," she said with a peck. "You sleep well?"

Before Brad could answer, Fletcher's boom sounded. "Time!"

❧

The crew gathered at Daisy Cottage, adding last-minute pumps of air to their tires and full water bottles to their frames. Judy laid out the day's agenda. "Well, folks, today's the icing on the proverbial cake. With the exception of the last ten miles,

118

this stretch is nothing but heavenly. Not to mention the most fascinating leg of the trail. It's thirty-five miles to New Franklin where our mansion rooms await. If you stick with me and toss out any 'rush mentality,' I know of some unlabeled detours you'll enjoy."

"Sounds fun, huh?" Brad said to Sonya.

"Yeah. . . Hey, where's your bike?" She only counted five.

"Don't worry about it."

Sonya squinted at her husband. "Aren't you riding? Are you okay?"

He turned away. *How odd!*

When Sonya sat on her bike, she immediately noticed that something was wrong. "Does anyone know why my feet don't reach the ground?" she called with an edge to her voice. "Someone messing with my bike?"

The group made lame attempts to suppress their smiles.

"What's going on? Hank, you're behind this!"

Hank held up his hands. "Not this time. I promise, I am completely innocent."

Sonya opened her mouth to ask Brad to lower the seat for her, but he had disappeared. Suddenly, the bacon-scented air smelled fishy.

"Now where's Brad?"

Fletcher said, "Gone."

Everyone laughed. Even Sonya cracked a smile. "No kidding. Where?"

"Right here!" came Brad's sunshiny voice. He walked his bike toward them—newly rigged with bar ends.

Sonya could not have felt more betrayed. Brad's dumb smile made the French toast turn *très mauvais* in her stomach. Appropriate words failed to come to her. She wasn't the swearing type, but temptation had a good argument for it at that moment.

Brad rolled his bike next to her and kissed her. If her seat wasn't so high, she might have stormed down the trail ahead of the others.

"Surprise!" Brad said.

"What is this?" Sonya frowned.

"Behold, your new bike."

"What?' Sonya's icky feeling broke apart into a million tingles. "You're giving me your bike?"

His smile looked adorable. "That's right. All yours. Forever. Or until the frame rusts away, whichever comes first."

"I. . .I. . ." Sonya lunged into his arms. "Thank you, honey. It's the most romantic thing I've ever heard of."

Over the palpitations of Sonya's fluttering heart, she could hear Hank's puppy-love-stricken voice. "Hey, Judy, can I go buy some of those handlebar thingies for Danielle?"

"You'll stay right here."

Audra called out, camera in hand. "Hey, you two—you've got another enlargement coming."

ða

As the group made their way to the trail, they took one last informal tour of Hartsburg. They passed the tall gingerbread-trimmed steeple and old stained glass windows of Hartsburg's church. A smattering of people wearing buttoned suits and knee-length coats sifted through the streets toward the church's door with the same countenance as the festival goers.

On impulse, Sonya yelled, "Stop!"

Brakes squeaked and gravel crunched. "What's wrong?" asked Brad.

"Nothing." She raised her voice for Judy's ears. "I know we have a long way to go today, but would you mind too much if I stepped into the church for a moment? It's Sunday. It would mean a lot."

"I don't have a rush mentality," Judy said. "Any of you all have it?"

Sonya observed a relaxed shaking of heads. "Thanks." She laid her bike on its side and held up one finger, a Mommy sign for *only a moment*. She ducked in the church door and stopped at the back of the sanctuary.

The sun's fingers touched the windows, quickening the

sacred rainbow images and casting kaleidoscope shadows on the pews' ends. The congregation transformed their hymnal's words to airborne expressions of their spirits. Sonya knew bits of each stanza, and she whispered the words with traces of prayers in between.

"Excuse me." A tall man touched her shoulder.

Sonya stepped out of the way for a family of three. Suddenly, she realized how out of place she must look with a plastic helmet topping off her fleece ensemble. She turned to go, but another woman entered.

Audra. She whispered, "I feel inspired, too."

Sonya wrapped her arm around her newfound friend's waist, and her embarrassment left. She said, "I have a lot to thank God for."

"We often forget," Audra said. They stood for another minute without words. Then Audra said, "I wish I could take a picture right now. I want to remember this."

"Do you go to church?"

"Never have."

"Why take a picture when you can have the real thing?"

Audra nodded. "Your question is one I could answer last Sunday: 'I have support already. I'm a good person. I recognize my spiritual side. I've done just fine without organized religion so far, thank you very much.' But your God's been tapping on my spirit the last couple days. And at this moment, I'm out of good excuses."

Sonya dropped her arm. "When God taps, see what He wants. It's always something to enrich our lives and make us better people." A Pharisee-like guilt bittered Sonya's words. Audra had opened Sonya's eyes to so many truths yesterday, acting as one of God's doormen to her. Was Sonya being self-righteous to think she had something more valuable than her friend?

No, if that's how she viewed it. They were two mothers trying to find their way through life the best they knew how. Two women, both with a history of mistakes and self-efforts. Both with the same offer of forgiveness. Good people, as Audra said. No different, except that Sonya knew the source of her goodness. She had accepted His gift.

Sonya said, "I think I know you well enough to say that you would love the life that Christ can give you. He's a truth teller, too."

"Oh yeah?" Audra said. "A truth teller, huh? Well. . ."

"Yeah, a truth and peace that you'll never find on your own. I know I seem naive at times. But I'd be a case without Jesus."

"I think you're wonderful. With you and Brad—yeah, I've seen some friction. But I've seen a love that goes deep. A love that never gives up."

Sonya was momentarily speechless. The choir sang a four-part litany. *Dear God. Let her know.* ". . .that's Christ." The end of Sonya's prayer formed on her lips. Did Audra hear it?

"Is it? A love that never gives up?"

"I couldn't have said it any better, Audra." Sonya peered at the cross. *Thank You for sharing Your truth.* "Well, we had better go."

Audra nodded.

Turning, Sonya noticed Brad in a back pew, head bowed. She slipped in next to him and squeezed his hand. He looked into her eyes, in silence. Suddenly she felt bound to him. She felt sure that they had reached out to Audra together.

ॐ

Being on the trail felt like going to a foreign culture for a week. The bikers no longer measured time in hours but miles, and a huge meal followed by a sound sleep were ideal payments for a hard day's work.

The river ribboned in and out of sight. Whether gazing at rushing waters and armies of bright, lush trees, Sonya saw beauty. Even the monstrous, algae-covered barges that dominated the waters had a soulful appearance. A man's adoration did that to a woman—it draped across her line of vision, making her look at all of life adoringly.

twenty-one

Before long, the autumn trees that lined the trail spread out in deference to sand-colored bluffs and the glossy river. The trail reminded Brad of the day he and Sonya biked apart, when she'd buddied up with Audra and when the cut on his leg still posed a threat. Yet this day, the colors seemed brighter, the water more lively, and the bluffs reaching even closer to heaven.

Judy called, "The Lewis and Clark Cave is coming up. . . just. . .about. . .now." She stopped.

Hank skidded to a halt, his eyes jumping back and forth. "Where?"

"Behind that sign," Judy explained.

"That sign that says, 'DO NOT ENTER UNDER PENALTY OF LAW'?" Hank asked, his voice dropping. "What good is a cave if you can't explore?"

He sat on the side of the trail. He took off a shoe and shook it. Fine gravel showered from the heel.

Brad yelled. "But you'd better watch that shoe of yours because—" Too late.

A tattered hound dog had bolted out of nowhere, grabbed the shoe between dripping teeth, and disappeared behind the "CAUTION" sign. "Hey!" Hank cried, standing on one sock foot. He hopped on the other foot toward the cave's mouth, hollering at the top of his lungs. "Come back here you mangy mutt! I need that shoe!"

Brad and Sonya looked at each other with concerned faces then burst out laughing.

"This is serious," Hank said with a boyish frown. He yelled again, "Come here, canine! Show your ugly face, dog food breath!" Only his words echoed back, taunting the redhead even more.

Amir stepped alongside the man whose complexion now matched his hair color. He pinched a piece of jerky between his gloved fingers. "Try this," he suggested. "The proverbial fly's honey with dog appeal."

Hank took it. "Thanks." He yelled back toward the sound of dripping water, "Mutt, dinner's on. Trade you a piece of meat for a shoe!" After a minute wait and a dozen more echoing drips, the beef jerky still dangled from Hank's fingers.

Brad felt Sonya pat his shoulder, and she gave him a wink. She called out, "You're doing it all wrong, Hank. Let's show him, Judy." She whispered her next words.

"I'll do alto if you'll go soprano," Judy said, laughing.

The two women melded voices in a love song that had topped the charts. "Baby, I'm missin' ya. Don't know if I can go. . ." Sonya held her hand to her heart while Judy gripped a fake microphone.

Brad chuckled as he stood back, watching the makeshift performers serenade a disobedient animal while a shoeless college kid chewed on jerky. Eyes widening, the college kid pulled the meat from his teeth and squatted down, holding it out.

But a few spirited chords later, round eyes reflected light like two white stars in the cave's belly. With measured steps, the canine thief teased the group by stopping at the cave's mouth. He didn't budge.

Hank shrugged and yelled, "Your loss, poochie!" And with exaggeration, popped the dried meat into his mouth.

Then, "Ouch. Ooh. Ouch!" Hank ambled over the gravel trail as if broken glass paved it. After he unzipped his bike bag, he pulled out a flashlight fit for a doll.

The song left Judy's lips, and she reverted to the part of a hard-nosed leader. "I'm not sure what you're thinking, but read the sign again, mister."

Hank ignored her warning. Tiptoeing back over the sharp rocks, he clicked on his flashlight. "Look out, Bowser. I'm coming in!"

After testing a maze of rocks, Hank waved his flashlight

and entered in. The thick darkness swallowed him. "It feels cool in here," came a far off voice. "I think I see my shoe." The resonating voice claimed a higher tone. "Good dog. . .now don't growl. I paid for those shoes at the mall. I have the receipt at home. . . . Hey!"

"What happened, Hank?" Judy called with cupped hands, her eyes scanning the trail for unwanted witnesses to her accomplice role in the cave break-in.

Hank yelled back, "Now that ugly dog has my flashlight." A growl drowned out Hank's last word.

Judy asked, "Does anyone else have a flashlight?"

Amir did, of course. Mr. Prepared-for-Anything. He chose different stepping-stones than Hank in his descent into the cave. "Coming, Hank. Stay put."

"What else am I going to do in a pitch-black cave with no shoes?" Hank said.

Amir answered with not a hint of humor in his tone. "Knowing you, I wouldn't risk a guess."

Fortunately, before a fellow biker discovered them, a wet, muddy Amir dawned from the darkness, as did Hank, balancing on slushy, shoe-covered feet.

"What is that, Hank?" Brad asked, noticing a box in his hands.

"I don't know. Here." He handed Brad the box as he climbed up the embankment. "Seems that Fido has quite a stash back there. Mostly trash. But this looked interesting."

Brad cracked the wooden lid with his fingernail and lifted a book from inside. It was ribboned and curled from the cave's humidity. Using a fingernail to separate the pages, he opened to a center spot. Music. Sheet music.

Judy cleared her throat. "I think you should turn that in to the parks department."

"I agree," Brad said. "I'll mail it off when I get home. But I want to page through it after it airs out." He shook out the excess water and gently tucked the antique pages in Sonya's new bike bag.

twenty-two

Sonya tilted her head as she stared at her husband. He seemed so eager to salvage the decaying paper that now dripped between Sonya's new bag's nylon seams. So strange.

Standing to put weight on her pedals, she rolled forward, the wet mutt following—still evidently enamored with her love song.

The trail traffic thickened even more, signaling that Rocheport must be around one of the next few bends. Sure enough, the trees cleared, and a new train station appeared to the right.

As soon as Sonya spotted the Happy Wagon, she ditched her bike, ran to a front seat, and sank in. The rest caught up and filed into the back seats. Fletcher returned, too. He reached to turn the key. "Ugh!" He let go and clamped his finger and thumb on his nose.

"It's Hank," Judy explained. "He went fishing. . .for his shoes."

"Shower!" Fletcher said, but Hank was already peeling dingy socks from his pruny feet.

Sonya wanted to presoak like never before.

❧

The Rocheport driving tour proved quaint. Bed-and-breakfast inns, antique stores, kind-looking restaurant fronts, art galleries, and bike shops. The van puttered to the west end of town to an antique shop full of sleepy cats.

Sonya and Brad stayed shoulder to shoulder as they window-shopped among the rows of Depression era glass. Sonya picked up a pink dish and stared at it. "I used to need all this *stuff* in my life to be happy. At least, that's what I thought. But I see now that as long as I have you and Maggie and my faith, it's all I need."

126

Brad was silent for a few seconds. Then he said, "That's a strong statement, Sonya. . .but I like the way it sounds."

With a nervous laugh, Sonya said, "Most things are easier said than done. At least you know where my heart is."

"Even though I've acted otherwise, I've never completely doubted it," Brad said. "I married you for that heart."

"Time to go!" Judy called, breaking off the conversation. "Can't finish until we start."

They loaded in the van again, trekked to the Trailside Café, and reclaimed their bikes that rested in the store's racks. Dozens of shiny bikes congregated with Sonya's. Rentals. Mountain bikes, hybrids, even a bicycle built for two.

Sonya dreamed about Brad showing the ultimate romantic gesture; he'd pull out the credit card at the trailside bike shop, rent the tandem bike, and do all the pedaling for the both of them.

But Sonya knew that that man did not exist. Not in Brad. Not anywhere.

The sweet man she *had* rediscovered put his arm around her shoulders as they rounded the corner to the bike rack. They passed the Happy Wagon again, and she almost broke loose to jump on board.

No, Sonya. You've come this far. Get ready, Booneville. I'm coming your way.

Sonya followed the line of bikers to the trail once more, but Audra was still in the Happy Wagon. "Audra, are you coming?" she yelled, wobbling on her bike as she looked back.

Audra kissed her hand and waved it, becoming smaller by the second and finally disappearing after they passed under a train tunnel. Sonya felt an urge to join her, but Brad said, "Where do you want to bike?"

"The middle," Sonya said, and they fell in between the other three. Sonya didn't want to, but she knew if she took the rear, the group would be stopping to wait at least every mile marker.

The trees still waved them on for a few miles. But then they spread out, only a few loyal hardwood cheerleaders were left to break the monotony of nothing but dry, harvested fields.

Sonya started to complain until Hank dropped back with other ideas. "Hey, have you two ever played the fabulous family name game? My brothers and I would play it in the car whenever we went on long trips. I thought it might shorten the ride a bit today."

Sonya smiled. "So you're getting tired, too?"

Hank produced a melodramatic look of shock. While he gripped his handlebars with one hand, he put the other to his chest and cried, "Who me? Never!"

"Sorry to suggest it," Sonya said. "Go on."

"We take turns naming fictional characters from the same family. For example, the Brady Bunch. I say Marsha, you say—"

"Alice," Brad spouted out. "Right! Whoever can't answer first gets a penalty point."

The game was unexpectedly hilarious. Before they knew it, Hank dropped out, and their game dissolved into tangents of Brad's and Sonya's childhood memories such as banana seats on bikes (which would have been pure torture had Sonya's bike still featured one that day) and action figures. Topics they hadn't talked about since they dated. More memories that they discovered they held in common.

Sonya laughed for thirty minutes until she caught herself. With Brad, the sound was foreign to her ears, the feeling unfamiliar to her lungs. She wondered how long since she and Brad had laughed so deeply and smiled so broadly together. Too long.

The more she thought, the more she realized that she had viewed their marriage story chiseled in stone: Written. Finished. Done. But now that dry, hard tablet had softened, and together, the couple carved new symbols into its clay. Ones that said change.

Ones that said hope. . .and a future.

Smiling meekly, Sonya let her eyes meet Brad's. He had grown quiet, too, and that, paired with the nondescript setting, filled Sonya with a strange peace.

twenty-three

Brad pretended to look at his speedometer, but Sonya's image lingered in his mind's eye. The look Sonya had just given made him shiver. *This bubbly, beautiful woman is my wife.*

What a breathtaking, miserable revelation. Breathtaking because he saw something new in her that he desired. Or more accurately, something *re*newed.

And something miserable because he couldn't—or wouldn't—recognize the abundance of those lovely qualities for so many wasted years.

Sonya's personality goes so much deeper than nagging words or hasty purchases. And when I am tempted to see her for those alone, I will remember how she added color to this long, drab bike ride on a cold October Sunday.

Now he knew what he had to do.

"Sonya. I have to talk to you about something."

Sonya looked at him, smiling, but as soon as she saw his sober expression, her mouth turned to an instant frown. Brad's confidence fell along with the corners of her mouth.

Why ruin a perfectly wonderful moment? His fear almost convinced him to change his mind. But an answer led him on. *Why? Because these next few minutes could help bring about even more perfectly wonderful moments in the future.*

He said, "I want you to come to work with me."

Sonya's face lit up again. "Really? I'd love to. I've thought about coming in time and time again. Like on your birthday. I imagined bringing in a balloon bouquet and baking a pan of brownies. You know, your favorite—the ones with the caramel and pecans inside. . ." She went into full detail.

A simple "yes" would have sufficed, but Brad was learning. "Yes" was plain vanilla, and Sonya was rainbow sherbet.

"Maybe you should save balloon bouquets for Maggie," Brad said. But with a newfound sensitivity, he added, " 'Cause I know she would go nuts over something like that." Yet the topic that he first intended to discuss still waited to drop. *Here goes.* "I want you to come to work for a different reason than parties and lunch dates." The next sentence was still locked up inside of Brad. He didn't have to say the words if he didn't want to. He looked at Sonya and noticed that her legs pedaled in synchronicity with his. They both must have chosen the same gear. Somehow, that connection gave Brad the added courage to say his next words. "I want you to meet Erin."

"Aaron? Is he new?"

"She. Is *she* new? No. She's been coming to Area for several months now."

All of a sudden, Sonya's cadence broke away from Brad's rhythm. She started to catch up with Hank, becoming so close that their wheels were in danger of overlapping.

"Sonya! Slow down! Wait!"

Brad's shout made Hank turn and look. He must have seen a look on Sonya's face that said, *Watch out! Nothing is slowing me down!* Because he started pedaling with all of his might.

"Sonya!" Brad persisted. "Come back here."

Either out of love or sheer exhaustion, Sonya slowed, and her bike fell back to spot parallel with Brad's. She turned to him, tears cutting through the trail dust that powdered her face, her chin trembling.

"I knew it!" she cried.

"No! No, it's not what you think. . . Well, it could have been. But it's not."

"Erin, huh? Is she the reason you've come home so late?"

Brad felt a lump in his throat. He croaked, "Partially. But hear me out."

Sonya began to gasp for air, and Brad suddenly wished they could have the trail to themselves. "Do you want to hang back?" he asked.

Sonya sniffled, wiped her nose with her sleeve, and nodded. After signaling, the couple stopped and dropped behind Amir.

After the group disappeared around the next turn, Brad said, "Now let's talk."

twenty-four

Sonya felt like a man in a suit had come to her house, announced that she was the winner of a million-dollar-sweepstakes, and then discovered that he'd knocked on the wrong door. *One. . .two. . .three. . .four. . .* Maybe counting each sweep of her feet would get her mind away from the pain of Brad's words that stung her ears.

Five. . .five. . . What number am I on? Amazing how emotions could turn her brain to mush. Even Maggie could count higher than she could now.

Five. . . Uhhh! How could *he? And I thought* I *was evil—sneaking bike rides!*

"Sonya, please listen," Brad said, all of his charm left a mile behind them.

"I don't know if I want to hear this!" she shouted.

"Trust me. You do," he answered.

Sonya yelled, "Okay, who *is* she?"

Brad's voice dropped. "She's a regular tennis player. Actually a player in more than one sense of the word. And evidently, she has some kind of unsolicited crush on me."

"And you?"

"I'll admit. She's very pretty—in a Barbie doll kind of way."

"Ugh!" Sonya interrupted. She made a note to put all of Maggie's fashion dolls in the trash compactor as soon as she returned home.

But Brad said, "Yeah. I agree with your assessment."

"You do?"

"At first, I was flattered." Brad admitted. "Erin listened to me as if every word I said was brilliant in itself. And then I would go home, and you would greet me with a barrage of complaints and a very unattractive frown."

Sonya swallowed. It was true. In a hushed tone, she said, "I'm sorry."

"I forgive you. I probably deserved it."

Sonya started getting over her initial shock. "Keep talking."

"I promise you this, Sonya. I hid out in the most creative places trying to avoid the woman. Usually in the men's locker room or my office. Once I even stood behind a heavyweight body builder."

That remark actually brought a laugh to Sonya's throat.

Brad smiled, too. "I have had some talks with Erin. The guys at the gym encouraged more. But God promised He'd never give me more temptation than I can bear. And I never did anything that I would be ashamed of. . .except maybe hiding behind that sumo guy."

After all of the berating Sonya had given Brad the last few months, she knew that many a man would have forgotten God and lunged right into this Erin's arms. Knowing what a prize Sonya had in the form of Brad's faithfulness, she heard the suited sweepstakes man knock once more. But this time, he'd found the right place.

"So that's why I want you to come to Area with me," Brad finished.

"And when I get there?"

Brad clinched his fist atop his handlebars. With a resolute tone, he said, "When you get there, we are going to march right up to Erin, and you are going to say—"

"I'm going to say, 'If I ever hear that you are talking to my husband again, I will personally see to it that the management reconsiders your membership privileges!' " Sonya nearly yelled the words.

"But *I'm* the management!" Brad said.

"No kidding. I'm very aware of that." Sonya thought about it for a moment. The confrontation was so unlike her. But with God's strength, she knew she could do it. "I would love to put that ultimatum in her face," Sonya decided. Her feelings of betrayal transformed to an even stronger sense of her own dedication to Brad. With satisfaction, she said, "The Kane family."

"What?"

"I've got a new challenge for the fabulous family name game," Sonya said. "The Kane family."

Hesitantly, Brad said, "Sonya. . .Maggie. . .and me?"

"And no Erin."

Brad nodded in revelation. "And no Erin. Never an Erin."

Sonya laughed. Gravel flew as she skidded out in front of Brad and put her arm out, hand down.

"What are you doing?" Brad called.

"Read the sign."

"Stop?" Brad asked. "Well, okay."

They did. Sonya dropped her bike to the ground and went to Brad's. She faced her husband, and unhooked his helmet. The helmet joined Sonya's bike on the trail floor, spinning like a top. Then Sonya looped her arms around Brad's neck and claimed him with a kiss.

twenty-five

The mile markers melted into each other. Finally Rivercene Bed-and-Breakfast was near, and they merged onto the street. Its smooth surface was glass beneath Brad's wheels after accustomed to four hours of gravel. His bike grew wings, almost self-propelling him and the others toward their beds for the night.

The path reverted to a chunky gravel driveway, and at the end, the Rivercene. The mansion rose before the tired group. Its angular walls offered a stately greeting—COME AND REST INSIDE.

The group shared awe-filled mutterings as they neared. Brad admired its masculine presence, coupled with romantic flair. At least a dozen banistered steps ascended to a covered porch that lined the house's face. Brad couldn't count all of the tall, slender windows that outlined the glimmer of the evening sun's reflection.

Fletcher waited by the van, the trailer's contents already strewn on the lawn. After putting up their bikes, Brad and Sonya grabbed their luggage and each other's hands, and they clomped up the porch steps. The front door, an elegant slab of black walnut, was cracked open.

Judy gave room assignments. The couple would sleep at the end of the second floor. They tiptoed in to meet with soft, leafy green walls. Those walls surrounded another of the marvelous fireplaces crafted from imported Italian marble. The bedspread was a fluffy, satin-like textile gleaming from the afternoon light that sifted between the openings in ceiling-to-floor lace curtains. They could stay for hours, but there was so much else to see.

Hank was not the only one who chose to explore this time.

Brad and Sonya poked their heads in door after door, finding each room radiating its own distinct personality—from mantle-length original paintings to Jacuzzis.

Judy loaded the crew in the van before she lost them to further expeditions, and they crossed the river bridge to a pizza place in Booneville.

"Our last dinner together," Sonya said quietly, as they slid into a booth. It was a comment that made the pizza parlor seem more like a funeral parlor.

An hour later, the unromantic van pulled up Rivercene's gravel drive for the night's stay. Sonya rested her head on Brad's shoulder. He stroked Sonya's forehead, brushing the hair from her eyes. He could feel her body relax even more.

"Who are you?" she whispered.

She sees it, too. "I'm that man wearing the ebony tux saying 'I do' in front of hundreds of people."

"Where were you all these years?"

Brad squeezed her shoulder. He felt a lump in his throat. "Missing out on what I had all along."

"Do we have to go inside?"

Who would have imagined that he and Sonya would ever deliberate between a cramped van that smelled like Hank's socks or a Victorian dream suite? "Only if we go in together," he said.

They did. Up the oak stairway with its walnut treads and hand-carved mahogany rail. Past the colossal wall tapestries and antique hall tables. Ending up at their room's doorway.

Brad twisted the key in the door. It opened.

"It's even more lovely than I remembered!" Sonya's eyes widened. She stepped in and sat on the bed, bouncing on the mattress like a little girl. She paused and looked around. "I'd love to crawl into bed, but I can't find my bike bag."

"Oh. I left it downstairs on the piano bench. Want to go down with me?"

"Well, okay." The two strolled past Amir and Audra's room on the way. Downstairs, Sonya spotted the vinyl bag and grabbed its strap. Brad started back.

"Just a minute," Sonya said, wandering the other direction. "I want to take another look." She seemed in her element—beauty admiring beauty. Even though she wore a turtleneck sweater and jeans, Brad was taken back. He sat on the piano bench and studied her.

She stroked the wooden piano. "What do you think has happened in the life of this old, cracked piano? Background for dinner parties? Dance music for balls? Christmas songs signaling that Emmanuel had come?"

Brad's mind grew fuzzy. He completed her thoughts. ". . . Little boys hitting sour notes as they learned scales? Piano teachers saying, 'Count with me—one and two and three'? Mother and son sharing the bench while they created a song together?"

Sonya stared at him. Then she said, "Why, yes. That, too. Those are wonderful images, Brad. How did you think of them?"

He shrugged. *I didn't think of them. They already happened.*

Sonya walked slowly away. She sat in a chair and gazed at the chandelier that dripped crystals from the ceiling. "And that chandelier. . .where do you suppose it's from? France? Austria? Sears?" She continued to speculate on the objects she saw: carved ceiling beams, rich tapestries, china as fragile as bubbles.

Instinctively, Brad lifted his legs over the piano bench to face the family of aged ivory keys. Like a piano student, he put his hands to them and produced a beautifully blended chord.

Sonya closed her eyes and leaned back. Brad shifted chords and produced another blend of notes. With eyes still closed, Sonya said, "That's nice. When did you learn to play that?"

"A long time ago," Brad said. He slid his hands from the keys and folded them in his lap.

Just like riding a bicycle. . .bicycle. . .bicycle. The words echoed in the silence. Were the melodies with their chord progressions and beats still waiting to be created by his dormant fingers? There was only one way to find out.

The antique piano needed tuning, but Brad still recognized the first few bars of "Lavender's Blue," a song he learned for his first recital. The simple melody sounded the same as it had years ago. Surprisingly, Brad fought the urge to weep, as if the suppressed music held a host of emotions captive until he released them again.

"Brad? That wasn't you. . .was it?" Sonya sat up and rubbed her forehead. "What else can you play?"

Brad faced the keys again. A lot of pieces. . .but Father Time had claimed chunks of the musical sequences. "Sonya, hand over your bike bag." She did, and the time-yellowed musical arrangements were piled inside, the Lewis and Clark cave relics, now almost dry. With utmost care, he smoothed the pages and leafed through them until a familiar arrangement caught his eye.

"This one's for you, Sonya." Again, his fingers met the ivory flats. He let them think for him, not conscious of the complex notes he played. All he knew was that a delicate melody filled the vast room. And he was the one bringing it to life.

He kept playing, less hesitant now, letting his music crescendo and whisper. Speeding and slowing with his emotion's whim.

A gentle warmth met his shoulders. The touch of his wife's hands. She put her face by his ear and peered over his shoulder at his waltzing fingers. A fresh spritz of apple scent. A feather-like touch of her hair. "You amaze me," she said.

Brad never dreamed he would hear the words coming from anyone other than his piano teacher or from stuffy relatives who couldn't tell the difference between a flat and a sharp. Especially not from a charming lady who called him her husband.

Her nearness now told him that she sensed the value of this talent, and as a result, it was important to her, too. This was just another way she had proved that her spirit beat in harmony with his.

She sat down next to him on the bench. "Please play another."

He did. . .a lullaby.

A rapid sequence of taps alerted them that someone was coming down the stairs. Brad stilled his fingers and saw Judy as she tiptoed in the room. "I didn't know we had a musician in the group."

"Neither did I," Sonya said.

Judy gave her a confused look. Then she said, "May I stay a bit? The music seems to complete the house."

Brad thought about it, then decided. "You're welcome to listen. What other music would you enjoy? Handel? Pachelbel?"

"Handel?" Sonya butted in. She looked at him with her head cocked. "You play Handel?"

"I think I can." With newfound confidence, Brad's fingers remembered part of a piece. They wedged only a few misled notes where they shouldn't have gone. The music floated up the stairs, luring another to the elegant room.

Judy placed two pink votive candles on the grand marble mantle, lit the little wicks, and clicked off the electric lights. The room filled with flickering shadows, making everyone's eyes twinkle and skin glow.

Brad continued his concert; the melting candles grew shorter and shorter. Occasionally, the women whispered to each other, but mostly, they just soaked it in. Brad wished his parents could saunter down the stairs and peer at him with proud eyes as they used to at his recitals. And then he realized that his heavenly Father, the one who gifted him in the first place, did listen—and was proud.

As Brad finished a selection from Grieg's *Peer Gynt Suite*, Judy stood and stretched. "Good night, you two."

"Good night." Sonya said, still at Brad's side. And then Brad and Sonya were alone again.

Sonya slid next to Brad on the bench and stroked the piano's keys. "Brad, why didn't you tell me about this before?"

"You knew I played."

"I knew you took some lessons, but I didn't know you *played*—not like *that* anyway. Why the secret?"

Brad thought back on the trail conversation he'd had with Amir. How liberating to admit the secrets, as Sonya just called them, to a man he hardly knew. How much more to the woman with whom he'd spend the rest of his life?

So he told her—about his coddling mother and the baseball team and his loneliness. And about the humiliating talent show, about his taunting peers.

And she responded by sliding even closer and meeting his lips with a soft kiss. A kiss that said, *Nothing's changed, Brad. I understand, and I still love you just as much as ever.* She said quietly, "I want to ask you so many questions, but I don't want to spoil this moment." They were composed words with no frills and no threat of unnecessary elaboration. Rich vanilla.

She's changing, too. We're both changing together. "Thank you, Sonya. I'd rather wait until tomorrow, too."

She blew out a breath. "I've always loved the sound of the piano. I wish that I could have taken lessons, but as they say, I can't carry a tune in a bucket."

"Oh yeah?" Brad asked, hiding a smile. He slid his hand over hers. "Put your pinkie right here"—he guided the finger to middle C—"and your other fingers like this." He placed them. "Now play."

A single chord trembled from the strings.

Brad delicately placed his hand on hers and his other hand on the keys. "Ready?" he asked.

He recalled *Lavender's Blue* once more, signaling Sonya to her parts, guiding chord changes without words, but with gentle touches alone.

It sounded more beautiful than Handel or Grieg. It was possibly the most beautiful song he'd ever heard.

They stopped with frozen stares, their hands still together. Brad said, "Do you think Judy would care if we borrowed those candles?"

Sonya shook her head. They each took a tiny glass globe, almost too hot to touch, and went upstairs by their light. There they placed the votive cups on their bedroom's mantel, the flickers doubling in a mirror backdrop.

The two crawled on the bed; Sonya rested on her side with her head on Brad's shoulder and her hand on his chest. "I love you, Brad."

He said. "I love you, too."

Brad was taken back by Sonya's reaction. Her body shook with sobs, and tears ran down her face, soaking through his shirt.

"Sonya? Honey, what's wrong?"

She couldn't answer. The tears kept falling, and Brad felt horrible. His mind scanned the night's events, trying to find a reason why she would suddenly break out in sobs.

"Sonya? Are those happy tears or sad tears?"

She sniffled and stopped for a moment. "A little of both, Brad. A little of both."

twenty-six

Sonya choked back her tears long enough to explain them. "I don't remember feeling more happy than tonight. When you wheeled out your bike and told me it was mine, I thought you couldn't top the moment. But you have. In so many ways. . . and I am scared."

"Scared?"

"And sad and lonely and. . .and. . .*scared!*"

Brad sat up and tilted her head so he could see her eyes. "I don't understand. This night's been perfect. It's what we dreamed when we said our vows. What God dreamed of from the beginning."

"That's just it! It's perfect. It gets no better. There is only one direction to go from here, and that's down." Sonya's tears won dominance again.

"Oh, honey!"

"It's true," she said, sniffling between phrases. "We're in a dazzling room with a promise of delicious, hot food in the morning. Not like home, Brad. No chipped nightstands and cereal here."

"So?"

"Are you listening?" She felt hope seeping out of her. "See? It's already happening. We're not on the same page."

"Sonya, relax. We've both changed. For the better. It will be different at home." The affirmation took the wind out of her sadness.

"Are you sure?"

"I'm sure about me. And even if you aren't, it won't change that fact."

Sonya wanted to move on with the romantic evening. But instead, new tears took her to the next looming disappointment.

142

"Brad, I don't think I can ever go back home."

He laughed, which made her reconsider her words. Then she asked, "What's so funny?"

"Nothing's funny," Brad said. "It's just that I've had the exact same thought."

"But we have to, Brad. Tomorrow is the. . .is the. . ."

"Last day?"

There, he said it for me. The last day. "Yes. And we will have to say good-bye to everyone. Who knows when, or if, we'll ever see each other again? This trip was more than I ever imagined—worth every leg cramp and busy afternoon I suffered in training for it. I've enjoyed it so much but never thought about it ending until tonight. Driving home seems so anticlimactic that my stomach feels queasy."

Brad was being inhumanly gentle so far, but a hint of impatience sneaked into his voice. "But that's tomorrow, Sonya. We still have tonight. Forget about tomorrow."

If only I could. Why can't I? "Okay," Sonya said, hoping that saying the words would help her act on them.

Brad leaned over and kissed her limp lips. "Sonya, you're not here."

"I'm sorry. I'm trying." She curled closer to him and let more tears work their way out. She pictured Audra taking snapshots of the rooftop bikes and heard Judy's voice joining hers in song as they pedaled down the trail. More images kept flashing in. . .Daisy Cottage chats, Pat's salad bar, pumpkin squares, hotel naps. . . Random, unconnected memories. And each one sent a new shock of sadness through her.

"I love you, Sonya," Brad kept saying, playing with her hair as he did.

"What's wrong with me? I wish—"

A shuffling noise broke her thought. Their bathroom door opened a crack. The candlelight cast just enough light to reveal a large animal slinking in on all fours.

Sentiment forgotten, Sonya sat up and pulled her legs to her chest. "Brad! What is that? Get it away!"

Brad swung his legs off the side of the bed, crouched down, and laughed. "Hi, Belle. Hi, good girl."

"Belle?" Sonya immediately recognized the golden lab they had seen earlier in the yard. She started to pet her when the door opened again. A short, lanky man walked in.

"Brad? Oh, I'm sorry." It was Hank. He waved. "Hi, Sonya. Good to see you." Then he crouched and patted his knee. "Hey, there, Belle. Come on, girl."

"Just what are you doing here?" Brad asked, a hint of amusement in his voice.

The third time I've wondered that. Somehow, he always seems to find our room, Sonya realized, this time grinning.

Hank motioned to the candles. "Evidently, I'm interrupting something. Sorry. Belle and I found a secret passageway in the house, and I wanted to see where it led. Now I know."

Brad laughed. "Well, now that you know. . .get out of here!"

"You don't have to remind me about that night at Plaza Five. I'm as good as gone. Belle, come now. You heard the man. We're not wanted here."

Sonya held her breath until the man and dog departed. Seconds later, she burst out laughing, and so did Brad. New tears fell, but these originated from a different place than the earlier ones.

"I'm not sure which scared me more, Belle or Hank," Sonya cried, wiping her eyes.

"Oh, that's not a tough call for me."

Sonya nodded. Simultaneously, they said, "Hank!" She passed Brad one of her tissues. "Well, God must have known I needed a good laugh."

"Yeah. It's not going to be *all* bad leaving everyone tomorrow."

Sonya counted on her fingers as she listed her thoughts. "No more midnight banana discussions. No more worries about Maggie. No more breathing sweat-laden Happy Wagon air. . ."

"And no more leg cramps!" Brad added. "See? You know we can hardly wait to get home, right?"

Sonya felt a lump in her throat threatening to drop to her

lungs and start her off again, but she swallowed and said, "Absolutely. But we *do* have one more night, like you said."

She gave Brad a gentle push toward the spot where Hank had appeared. "Just to be safe, go lock that door."

❧

Fletcher's knock disturbed Sonya's exhaustion-fueled sleep for the last time. Here she was, waking up without the scream of an alarm in a glistening room next to a beautiful man. Could she freeze this moment like almond cheesecake so she could take a bite sometime later when the craving hit?

Yes, in her memory.

"Brad," she whispered. "Thanks for. . ." *everything*. There were too many particulars to list.

Brad kissed her. "God's here, isn't He?" came his first words.

Sonya hadn't realized it consciously, but yes, she could sense His presence now. Did Brad have any idea how many prayers she had scattered before them like rose petals on the trail? She said, "He's here. I've been asking Him to use this trip to make our marriage relationship strong."

"Me, too."

How funny it seemed. . . She and Brad had both been talking to God, asking him for help. God must have held back His kind laughter, as Sonya did just before Maggie's birthday last year. The little girl kept begging for a doll bed, but Sonya had tucked one, still boxed, in the attic weeks earlier. She tried not to give any hints, any clues that Maggie's request had already been taken care of.

Brad said, "I think He's the one we need to thank, more than anyone."

Sonya nodded.

With that, their voices recessed into the quiet, though Sonya knew that God was receiving a silent thanksgiving in stereo.

❧

An hour later, the couple clomped down the stairs and met the others at a long, cloth-covered table. Audra still wore a thick robe, and Hank's hair hadn't gotten the consideration that

Sonya's had. *Like family,* Sonya thought. *Free to be ourselves. Knowing appearances won't change anything.*

Belle wandered to Sonya's side, nudging her elbow. "Well, hi there, Belle. You're a lot less scary in the light."

The food made a train around the table. Rich sausages, blueberry-jeweled muffins, and the house specialty, Finnish pancakes.

Judy gestured for some butter then announced, "Speaking of Finnish, we're almost done with our mission. By dinnertime, we will have biked across most of Missouri. What a great accomplishment for you all. After breakfast, we'll bike through Booneville and start our ascent to Sedalia."

Ascent? That doesn't sound promising.

"No more rivers or bluffs, but lots of lush trees to tunnel under. The quaint towns are small and far apart. At Sedalia, Fletcher will clear out the trailer, and you'll be free to go back to your kids—or your roommates. The shuttle will come within the hour to take you back to St. Charles."

Sonya slouched over her plate. Her eyes met with Audra's, who looked on the verge of tears. Neither dared say a thing. They knew where that would lead.

She knew that on any other occasion, a second helping of Finnish pancakes would have been a difficult temptation to resist. Today, though, she was lucky to eat the two she took.

God, why is my heart still so heavy? She felt as if she had woken from a marvelous dream to discover that it was over.

A quiet voice seemed to say, *Sonya, though dark times will come and go like shadows, the dream doesn't ever have to end.*

twenty-seven

As Brad packed an extra spare tire in his bike bag, he knew that a locomotive could not keep him from finishing the Katy Trail. The man sprouted wings on his trip to Cloud Nine with Sonya last night. His terrific mood made the word *invincible* self-descriptive.

Judy's last "Ready?" brought a whooping shout from Brad instead of his usual silent head nodding.

They pedaled in spurts onto the four-lane highway and followed the shoulder to the bridge they had driven over the night before. After crossing it, Brad read storefront signs along Main Street that gave this town 1950s appeal.

The old Booneville train station waited at the bottom of a steep decline. Unlike the other stations—typically privy-sized that once stated *All aboard*—this stone-faced monument once *boomed* the words.

All aboard. All aboard on the last train to Sedalia.

After last-minute swigs of water, the group formed a draft line at the trail gate. Single file, they pedaled on without conversation, relishing a last fling with the Missouri autumn.

Gears clinked more frequently than past days. The formerly flat trail protested Brad's attempt to leave, too, its upward slope making continual work, continual burn for his leg muscles. Visibly, the degrees of inclines were imperceptible. But when Brad's muscles felt aflame, he clicked the gearshift with his thumb, forcing the oily chain to drop another notch.

Finally, signs of civilization broke the never-ending rows of trees: the trademark train station. Towering flagpoles and tiled rooftops. A tar-covered lot leading to a grocery store, the Happy Wagon already stationed upon it.

After another water break, Judy pumped up the group

again. "Clifton City is our last stop before Sedalia. Twelve miles, then nine. We're right on schedule."

Brad lifted his foot to push off. A thrust. A roll. Unexpected resistance. "Oh, no," he said, pulling at a stray wire. He tested his bike, discovering that the yanked wire had shifted his brake pads. "I'm right behind you. This won't take long. Go on, everyone."

After declining several offers for help, Brad watched the group roll off. All, that is, except one.

She threw her arm around his waist. "Be my partner for the last twenty miles?"

"Longer than that," Brad said with a friendly kiss.

&

"We'll never catch up," Sonya said as Brad did a final tweaking on his brakes.

"We are so buff, just watch us!" Brad took pride in labeling his wife that way now.

Sonya's mouth curled up on one side. Brad tipped up her chin, and the kiss he planted made her frown turn up completely. Her eyes smiled, too.

"Ready?" He asked Sonya the rhetorical question as she straddled her bike. After bouncing over a few tufts of grass, the couple's bikes met the familiar vibration of the pebbly trail.

"What do you think they'll do with all that leftover food in the coolers?" Brad asked, not really caring about the answer. He smiled to himself, contented that he actually *wanted* to hear Sonya's long-winded speculations.

"Freeze it, give it to a homeless shelter, eat it. . . ," she answered. "Maybe they'll divvy it out as souvenirs. Don't know. . . Hey, those apples were fantastic, didn't you think? Really crunchy and sweet, not mealy like Red Delicious. What kind did the bag say? Fuji? I always thought that Fuji was a mountain in Japan, but I'm sure they didn't pick them in. . ."

As suspected, Brad's wife created an essay from an uncomplicated question. He tried to imagine her in her younger days, interviewing television guests. She'd been poised and professional. Her elaboration was concise and relevant there.

Now he saw her ramblings with him as a love language, not a weakness. She was not concise, relevant, or poised. Rather, intimate. . .soul baring—

Bang!

The sudden explosion cut Sonya short and echoed in Brad's ears. And though Brad tried to keep pedaling, he simply couldn't.

twenty-eight

The explosion's echo seemed to shake Sonya from the very trail. Her husband's pace slowed until he finally stumbled off his bike. "Brad!" Sonya threw hers to the ground and ran to his side. "Brad, are you okay? Was that a gunshot? It sounded like a gunshot!"

Brad dropped to a crouched position.

"Brad!" Sonya squatted next to him, confusion swirling her thoughts.

He lifted a spiked object from the chalky pebbles and held it out for her to see. "Thorns. That's what you heard. Looks like I have a flat."

Sonya let out a long, relieved breath.

Brad stood and unzipped his bag. He loaded his hands with all kinds of little tools molded of metal and plastic, and he looped his spare tube around his neck.

"This should only take a minute or two," he said, starting to pry the tire from the rim.

"Have you ever changed a flat before?"

Brad kept working. "I know what to do."

Another question evasion. The man could avoid them so well when he couldn't admit weakness. *I can't expect that everything has miraculously changed.*

Brad took the wheel from the frame and sat on the ground. He propped it between his knees and used a tool to pull the tire from the rim. "See, Sonya. I've got it under control."

"Good." *So far.*

Then Brad pulled the tube from the rim and tossed it to the side. The other tube came off his neck, and he gave it a couple of good tugs.

"Aren't you going to break it that way?" Sonya asked, wanting badly to jump in. "I didn't see Amir do that."

He took a deep breath and blew it out his nose and simply said, "Please, Sonya." He wedged part of the tube in the rim and began to pull the rest of it into the groove. As soon as he reached the other side of the tube, the original section had popped out.

"Can I help hold it?" Sonya asked.

"Let me try again, okay?"

Why is he being so stubborn? Sonya's stomach felt tight, her muscles on edge. The distance from the others was widening by the minute.

Brad tried again.

Once more. No luck.

"Maybe if you use that tool thingie, you could get it on," Sonya suggested.

"I *am* using the tool thingie!"

"Yeah, but maybe you need to hook it under and flip it around. Like this. . ." She showed him, charades style.

"That doesn't look right," he moaned. Brad ignored her and tried again. The same way he did last time. With the same outcome.

He looked at the bike with fiery eyes and tossed the flat tool to the ground. "Okay, Miss Fix-a-Flat. Go ahead and try."

Sonya leaned down and picked the wedge from the dirt, glaring.

Brad frowned and kicked the powdery trail floor.

Sonya angled the tool and started the wrestling match between the tube and the rim. She yanked as hard as she could, but the rubber ring didn't want to budge. Brad stood nearby, his arms folded. Sonya grunted. With one last tug, she managed to accomplish something different than Brad had; she drove the wedge right through the rubber tubing. "Oops."

Sonya took her turn to toss the wedge down. "I'm glad you have another spare in your bag. You do have two, right?"

"Yes. I *did* have two. Now I have only one!"

Yes, vacation is definitely over. Welcome back to real life. Sonya shoved the depressing thought away and tried to think of the task at hand.

Brad went through the stretch, pull, wind, grunt routine again. This time, he succeeded in replacing the useless tubes. Using his shirttail, he wiped his forehead and lip and stood up. "Finally. Now we can go."

"I think that first one was defective," Sonya said.

"Yeah, maybe so." Brad said, not looking at her.

They mounted their bikes and pumped up the newest incline, their hearts and lungs objecting to starting up again so suddenly and so vigorously. Brad seemed focused on the course ahead, obviously not wanting to make—or listen to—any kind of conversation. Sonya gritted her teeth. *Okay, God. I want to trust You, but I'm not feeling very hopeful right now. Is anything different? Were we just caught up in the excitement of new surroundings and the freedom of having no responsibilities? When we get home, will—*

Bang!

Another gunshot imposter. Another wayward thorn.

Brad hopped off his bike, pushed it over, and threw up his hands. "I can't believe this!"

Sonya felt proud of herself as she posed an idea. "I have a spare tube."

Brad shook his head. "Too big. Our bikes use different sizes."

"Oh, boy."

"Oh, boy, is right. Well, we had better start walking."

Sonya suggested, "I could go for help."

"You'll never catch up with them. Then what if something happens to you? No. We had better stick together."

"Okay." Sonya swung her leg over her bike frame and began pushing it along by the handlebars. How long would it be until they reached the next meeting point? An hour? Two? She kept her lips pressed tightly together until she couldn't stand it any longer. "Brad, I have just one more thing to say."

"Just one? Promise?"

Sonya felt heat rise in her face. "No, actually I don't promise! Why am I forced to feel as if I have to ration my words around you?"

"When have you ever rationed your words?" he answered.

"All the time. Don't your realize that? I have so many thoughts swimming in my head, but I just push them down sometimes because you act as if I'm torturing you when I don't."

Brad picked up his pace.

"Brad, are you listening?"

"Yes. Did you ask a question? Do I have to give a paragraph essay in response to all of your complaints?"

"You don't. And it's not all complaints. Like last week. I told you about Maggie's school project, and after two sentences, you lost interest."

"Maggie is a whole other subject. But yes, sometimes you just give me more than I care to know."

"But *I* care about it." Sonya knew her statement was followed by an implicit *you should, too. But why don't you?*

"Sonya, listen to me. Do you care about my O2 max or which sanitation chemicals Area Gym uses? Is it important to know when gym memberships are two for one? Does it matter to you when I gave the van an oil change?"

"Well, no. Except the oil change. My sister's engine block cracked once, and I don't want that to happen again."

Brad rolled his eyes, still walking faster than Sonya cared to.

Maybe this would help. "Brad, I was talking to Audra and Judy. I understand myself better now."

Brad stopped and turned. "You want to fill me in?"

"Yes, I do. Maybe I do talk too much, but it's understandable. My words have always been my crown of glory. At school, at work. So after we got married, and you started to yawn at my monologues, it said only one thing to me. I'm not important."

Brad's words were clipped. "That's not true."

"I feel like it. So sometimes I keep talking. To get a reaction.

Any kind of a reaction."

"And my irritation meets that goal?"

"No. But that's when I just give up and realize I'm not getting anywhere."

"Wouldn't it just be better to quit while you're ahead?" asked Brad.

"Feeling ignored is hardly being ahead."

"You have to understand my side, too," Brad began.

Sonya resisted but found the resolve to pray silently. *Open my mind to the truth.* "Okay, Brad, what side is that?"

Brad froze. "Not now."

If not now, then when? Avoidance tactics in action once again. Sonya's spark of hope was smoldering. "Fine, Brad," she complained. "Maybe you'll tell me before Maggie graduates from high school."

"No! Sonya, stop. Don't go any farther." He made a barrier by putting his arm across her chest. "I just don't think this is a good place to have a heart-to-heart."

"Why not?" A round, corrugated metal tunnel covered a length of the trail. In it, Sonya saw what made Brad become instantly rigid. A thick, depraved-looking snake.

"Back up. Very slowly." Brad whispered.

Without a word, they did. They backtracked until the tunnel looked like a pinhole.

"Was it poisonous?" Sonya finally asked as her heart raced.

"I'm not sure. I think so."

"So what now?"

"Let's do what you're so good at."

"What?" asked Sonya. "Scream? Panic? Come up with ideas that won't work?"

"Talk."

Sonya laughed. "I can do that!"

twenty-nine

Brad turned from the tunnel, from the snake. "So where were we?"

"Your side. Let's hear it," Sonya said with her head tipped.

"Okay." *Where to start?* "Do you know how it was for me? Unlike you, I was the quiet kid at school. Just a few friends from band. Alone a lot."

"Oh, I'm sure it wasn't that bad," Sonya said. "Everyone likes you."

"Maybe now. But while you had the student body around your little finger, they were putting formaldehyde frogs down my shirt."

"Sounds lonely."

Brad thought. "The frog part, yes. But generally, I liked being alone. I felt pressured to be like everyone else, even though I wasn't. I felt. . ." He paused. "I learned to depend on myself. And later, thankfully, on God."

"That's good, Brad. I worry too much, but many times when we were first married, you were a rock. I'm stronger in my faith because I've seen you model that."

Brad felt humbled. He still took control of situations on his own strength, in his own time, too often. He continued. "I found refreshment in the quiet times. The alone times. When I was with people, I felt as if they were looking down their noses at me. I still do at times." He added, "Even with you."

Sonya withdrew her hand. "But, Brad, I am not the one distancing. You are!"

"Because you can't accept me the way I am!"

"Which is?"

"Alone. I need to be alone. Your constant chatter makes me stressed."

Sonya huffed out, "I'm irritating again, huh?"

"Not half as much as your mother!" Brad cried, his emotions rising to the surface for an encore.

Sonya gasped.

"There. I said it. Sonya, that woman sucks the life out of you. Talk about having someone wrapped around her little finger. She brings out the worst in you."

Sonya stood, "Okay, Mr. Psychiatrist. Tell me what I'm supposed to do. I'd rather be irritating than insensitive."

Brad stood and took Sonya by the shoulders. "Honey, I'm not being insensitive. I'm protecting you. And us. When you married me, you vowed to put our relationship before your family. But your mom has convinced you that I am the bad guy here. Sure, she needs you, Sonya. But she won't wither and die without your constant attention. We don't have to suffer because of her."

Sonya slumped. She didn't seem to know what to say.

Brad asked with a soft voice, "Are you okay?"

"I don't know," Sonya answered. She sat again. "I have always been responsible for Mom. I feel indebted to her."

"You are a loyal daughter. This planet needs more like you. But catering to her weaknesses won't help anyone. She'll hate the change at first. But over time, it will get better. . .for all of us."

"I'll have to think about it," Sonya said, trembling. "When she, or you, are upset or displeased, I try to make it right. I'm always trying, but I can't seem to do it. I can't seem to win your approval."

"You can't *make* me happy, Sonya."

"See? You won't let me."

"No. I hate to say it, but you are not my whole life, hon."

Sonya's shoulders began to shake, and tears spilled down her cheeks. "I know. It hurts so bad. . .so bad."

Brad tried to feel compassion, but he cringed instead. "Do you feel like your happiness depends on me?"

"Sometimes," she sniffled. "You and Maggie."

What a heavy responsibility to bear. Now he knew why he'd felt smothered for so long. "Have you always felt this way?"

Sonya pulled a tissue from her pocket and blew her nose. Her bloodshot eyes stared at the clouds. "Well, no. Maybe. I want to put everyone in neat and tidy boxes, but I can't, especially now with a child. Brad, I can't do it all." Sobs broke through. "But you expect me to. You never help out."

Brad felt his jaw tense upon hearing the word *never*. He pictured his dimple-faced daughter smiling at him, then turning to her mother when she needed something. "No. You're not expected to do it all. Not even. I just know you can do it better than me, that's all. You're a good mom, Sonya. So good that when I step out on a limb with Maggie, you'll find a million things wrong. I love Maggie with all of my heart. You know that. But I. . .I. . ."

". . .feel incompetent?" Sonya asked.

The words stung. But somehow, Brad knew that was not Sonya's intention. "I guess you could put it that way."

"You think if you take some responsibilities, I will criticize you."

"That's right," Brad said, actually feeling heard. "It's happened before."

"That's what Audra said." Brad thought he heard Sonya mumble the words under her breath. Then she said, "What if I let you do it your way? No corrections."

Just what Brad had always wanted to hear. He thought if that day would ever come, he would feel a huge burden fall from his shoulders. But strangely, he felt a wave of fear. "That would be great. But," he sighed. "I don't know if she'll accept it."

"Like you said with Mom, she'll probably hate it at first. But in the long run, it's better for everyone."

"Don't go throwing my words back at me," Brad said, finally feeling a grin spread across his face.

But Sonya simply stared at the clouds again.

"I'm glad we got all of that settled," Brad said, looking up, too. The sky was a tent of gray with a sliver of blue in the distance.

Sonya bit a nail.

"Aren't you?" he asked.

"Brad, who are we fooling?" Sonya cried. "We come on a beautiful trail with no responsibilities, and we have a few romantic moments. It's nice, but reality waits—as close as tomorrow. Sure, we talked through some issues, but for every one we squared away, I'm sure there are ten more just waiting to come to the surface. This whole trip, it's been that way. I think, 'Hey, we're doing okay!' and then—*Bang!* Another problem. I don't know. We have so many differences. I'm still afraid. . . . Afraid we'll go the rest of our married days battling problem after problem. We'll never get it figured out."

Sonya's face showed worried wrinkles. For a moment Brad felt fear seize him, too. *God, I know You want the best for our marriage. But Sonya's words are discouraging me. Do we have a leg of hope to stand on? Can we have a marriage that's everything You designed?*

Suddenly, Brad said, "Bingo!"

Sonya's body jerked from surprise. "What?"

"You're right. You're absolutely right." Brad stood and extended his hand to pull her up. "Let me show you." He led her to the blue rental bike. The one with the flat tire. He pointed. "What's this?"

"Is this a trick question? Last time I looked, it was a tire."

"Right," Brad said. "A flat tire. But it can be fixed. The bike will serve its purpose again. But that tire will keep going flat. Holes, slashes, cracks. All kinds of problems. It's tough when it happens, but you fix them and keep going."

"I see. Like our marriage?"

"Like our marriage. We *will* have more problems, Sonya. You can count on it. When Maggie gets to be a teenager, if you ever go back to work, or I change jobs, or we have to move, these situations will set the stage for a myriad of new obstacles. They will never end. But we can submit to them or keep patching them up and go on."

"Hmm."

Another thought hit Brad. "We knew one of us might get a flat on the trail, didn't we? We brought tubes and tools so we'd be ready. But were you worrying about it the entire trip?"

"No," Sonya said.

"We enjoyed the ride. We can do the same—you and me. We may hit a thorny spot, but if we trust Christ to help us patch things up, we'll come out just fine." He put his arm around Sonya. "And we will. We'll be just fine."

Sonya put her head on Brad's shoulder, and this time, the tears fell in torrents.

Hope waved its flag of victory.

❧

Brad and Sonya found their places on the gravel again and held each other, not talking. Sonya's body felt warm and full of life.

"You know what patches marriages the best, right?" Sonya asked. Brad could feel her chest expand and contract with his words.

"What? Kisses? Guilt gifts? Forgiveness?"

Sonya laughed. "I didn't even think of guilt gifts, but that would be nice. . . . Yes, all of those are good, but I was thinking more of praying. It's what brought us here in the first place."

Brad nodded. "You know, I think we've handled prayer the same way we've handled everything else. Solo. His and hers. I want that to change."

Sonya said, "I do, too."

Brad closed his eyes and squeezed Sonya's hand. She began, "Dear Lord, thank You. . .for the last week, for all the lessons learned. For hearing us and being so true to Your nature—a healer. One who patches things up so they work again."

Brad couldn't help but open his eyes. Distractions from God did not exist here. All of his surroundings reminded him of his Creator—the autumn leaves, the bluing sky. The wife. Once a derogatory term in his mind, now a word of acclaim. "Yes,

Lord," he said, looking at this wife of his with her head bowed so reverently. "I know that Sonya and I can be dense sometimes. We forget what You can do. . .what You have done. But please, stamp this day in our minds and in our hearts. And if we forget, help us remind each other. You can fix a flat marriage. It's never beyond repair."

"As long as we keep asking you to fix it," Sonya said.

"Yes. Help us not to try it on our own. Forgive us for making such a mess of things at times. We—"

"Hello!" came a voice from the direction of the tunnel. Brad and Sonya looked up.

"Amir!"

Sonya stood brushing clinging rocks from her legs. "I'm so glad you came. We had a flat. Well, Brad had a flat. We tried to change it and popped the first tube. . ." She told it all.

Amir hopped off his bike. "So the thorns discovered your bike, too? Judy's back tire found one just past the tunnel. They're like shag carpeting this time of year."

"Where is everyone now?" Brad asked.

"At Clifton City Gas and Grub. We started to worry, so I came looking for you. I'm glad your hold up was caused by the thorns and not by a snake bite." Amir held up an orange canister with a tiny hose coming out of its top. "I brought you this."

Brad stepped over to him and took it. The label said, FAST FLAT FIX. "How does it work?"

Amir pointed to the directions. "Attach it to your nozzle. It fills your tire long enough to get you to the next spot."

"Hmm." Brad looked at Sonya. Sometimes even a temporary fix would do the job. In tires, in marriage. Sometimes you have to trust without everything being in perfect order.

Brad let Amir do the honors. The canister hissed as it filled the withered tube with foam. Amir popped it off and said, "Ready!"

Brad smiled. "Thanks, pal."

The three set off toward Clifton City. The ominous snake had long left its place in the trail tunnel, and fifteen minutes later, the sun's reflection off of a blue van guided them to the Gas and Grub.

Amir unhooked his gloves and said, "Let's go find the mechanic."

Brad parked his bike next to a silver one he recognized as Audra's, and the three latecomers walked in. With the reception they got from the others, Brad was surprised that a news crew wasn't lurking in the corner waiting to flash their picture.

"Are you guys okay? We were worried sick." Audra threw her arms around Sonya's neck.

Judy raised a can of lemon-lime soda toward them. "Let me guess? Another thorn victim?"

Amir returned with a man in overalls streaked with grease and sweat. "Here's our man," he said.

Brad started toward him, but a thick, dark arm created a barrier. It was Fletcher. "Freeze!" he said as he gestured to an open stool.

Brad had more than a dozen reasons not to argue with the man. "Thanks."

Sonya and Hank surrounded him on either side. Hank placed three bottles of strawberry-ice Sports Solution on the counter.

The woman behind the counter looked up from some paperwork to the drinks and mumbled, "You want those?"

"Not sure," Hank replied, lifting one above his head. He tilted it back and forth, looked up inside, then did the same with another.

Sonya beat Brad to his next question. "What *are* you doing, Hank?"

"Trying to win something. There are prizes written in these lids, and if you tilt them just right, you can see what they say." He put down the third bottle and pushed it forward. "I'll take this one," he said.

The sandy-haired owner rolled her eyes at him and said, "Two dollars."

"But it says one dollar on the fridge."

"Two," she repeated. "And don't let me see you cheating again."

"Okay," Hank said, pulling a bill from his bike bag. He unscrewed the lid and took a swig.

Suddenly Brad felt thirsty. As he walked toward the glass refrigerator, he asked Hank, "So what did you win?"

"Got myself a free sundae," Hank said proudly, holding up the lid as if Brad could read it from that far away. Behind him, the owner peered at Brad through slitted eyes.

Brad held up both of his hands in surrender. "Don't worry, ma'am. I'm not planning on looking under any lids. I'm just thirsty." He asked Sonya, "Do you want anything?"

"Cool-blue Sports Solution," she said.

He pulled out two.

"One dollar," the owner requested. Hank opened his mouth in protest, but the woman shook her finger at him. "Sonny, you don't have a word to say that won't convict you further."

The sweet, cold drink was air conditioning to Brad's muscles. But Hank sat with a melodramatic disgruntled look and whispered, "Did you win anything, guys?"

Sonya squinted into her lid. "It says, *Sorry. You're not a winner.* How about you, Brad?"

Brad finished swallowing the last drop in his bottle before he flipped his lid to look. He expected the same words as Sonya's but instead. . ."I won!"

Hank grabbed Brad's wrist, pulling the winning lid in reading range. "You won? Look at that—a night's stay at Motel Nine. No way!"

"Let me see!" Sonya cried, holding out her hand.

Brad handed her the plastic lid. He thought back on their lodging the last four nights: Lavina's Place adorned with ivory lace and shelves of books; the capital hotel's king-sized beds and room service; the Skye with its antique beds and thick robes. And finally, last night's stay at the elegant Rivercene. That would never be a lost memory. He said, "I think I'm spoiled now. I can hardly bear to sleep at a place like Motel

Nine after the Rivercene. It's in the same league as a dormitory now."

Sonya gripped the lid. "I don't know, Brad. I think the roommate's more important than the room."

Brad put his hand over her closed fist. "Yep, I agree. You want to be my roommate?"

"Forever," she whispered.

Brad gently slid the lid from her fingers and zipped it safely into his pouch. Sonya was right. Whether Plaza Five or Motel Nine, as long as he could wake up and feel Sonya next to him, he was at the right place.

Fletcher and the Gas and Grub man clamored back in the front door.

"All fixed," Fletcher announced.

Judy waved the group over to the huddle. She said to her crew, "It's later than usual, so we'd better get going, Only nine more miles to Griessen Road."

"Sedalia!" Fletcher said with more enthusiasm than Brad could remember him ever showing.

Another shadow crossed Sonya's beaming face. "Nine miles and it's over," she said, with a catch in her throat.

"The trip might be. But, honey, the rest is only starting."

thirty

The trees and the gravel had flowed into Sonya's dreams the last couple of nights. She could see the terrain perfectly when she closed her eyes. She didn't care if she saw more of the same today. Instead, she dropped to the tail of the strand of bikers, memorizing their forms and quirks so thoroughly that a police artist could draw photo-like portraits from her descriptions. *I don't want to forget any of them. I don't want to leave.*

When Sonya fell to the rear, Brad slowed and joined her.

"Don't want to get separated from my partner," he said with a wink. Much different than a month ago.

The trail continued its uphill grade. At the bottom of every hill, Sonya told herself that what goes up must come down. But when she reached the top, another menacing hill emerged. "Remind me to do this trail backward next time."

"Next time?" Brad asked.

Sonya hadn't thought when she said the words. They were simply part of an expression. . .weren't they?

Brad pressed again, "Do you want to ride the trail again someday?"

"Well. . ." She paused. "Yes. I do. Maybe not with Katy Escapes. But by ourselves. . .we could take abbreviated trips. A weekend here and there."

Brad smiled, looking deep in thought.

"What's going on in that mind of yours?"

"Great idea, Sonya. A month ago I never thought we'd be having this conversation. You. . .me. . .taking a trip alone and enjoying it. Doing something *active* and enjoying it! But now I think we could actually pull it off." His grin spread even wider. "Let's go next week."

Sonya giggled. "We definitely don't have the money for that."

"I agree. One more problem, though."

"What's that?"

"What if we get a flat? No Amir. No Happy Wagon. We can only take so many protein bars for survival."

Sonya clicked her tongue. "I guess that we'll have to fix it ourselves."

"Guess so."

"We better—"

"Better what?" Brad probed.

Sonya almost didn't finish her next thought. Would Brad feel criticized or think she was mothering? But she tried out the good-natured comment anyway. "Better buy a plenty-pack of spare tubes, huh?"

Her husband laughed. And with that, she knew they could do it.

When they reached the last mile marker, the chatter and trail songs degenerated into a ruckus of hoots and hollers. Fletcher stood at the end of the trail, hand extended to congratulate the team on their accomplishments.

"You did it," Brad said to Sonya. "I didn't think I'd be saying that, but I'm glad I was wrong." A second later, they whizzed past Fletcher, slapping his up-turned hand. Yes, she had done it!

❧

"Over two hundred miles and we didn't lose a soul," Judy said as the six gathered around the dusty, blue Happy Wagon for parting thoughts. "You were a great group, and I will miss each and every one of you." Judy's smile looked pasted-on. Her words seemed prerecorded, too formal.

Sonya broke in. "I'm gonna miss you, too, Judy." She looked around. "All of you."

Audra nodded. Even Amir's eyes glistened.

But Judy continued as if she didn't notice. "Fletcher's unloading your gear, and a shuttle bus arrives in about thirty minutes to take you back to your cars."

Sonya's feet wobbled on the gravel as she stepped toward her leader and wrapped her arm around the woman's shoulders. She called out to the group. "Judy's the best. Don't you think so?"

They did. Between Audra and Amir's claps, Hank's whooping, and Brad's vigorous nodding, their leader couldn't miss it.

"I guess I can relate to a doctor. 'Don't get close to your patients,' they say. 'Don't allow yourself to have personal relationships.'" The once-composed woman started to sniffle. She said, "I'd make a rotten doctor."

Now Audra surrounded Judy from the other side. "But you make a great trail guide."

Hank said, "Yeah. We love you, Judy!"

The teary-eyed trail guide wrapped her arms around Sonya and Audra and said, "I love you, too. All of you. I wish you the best." She smiled a courageous smile. "Now as I was saying, if we don't get moving we'll miss the next shuttle."

"There's more than one?" Audra asked.

"Yes. One leaves every two hours."

Audra looked at her sports watch. "It's practically five. Dinnertime. Why don't we get something to eat and take the shuttle after this one?"

"I'm all for that," Hank cried, patting his stomach.

Hungry or not, Sonya couldn't think of a better idea.

thirty-one

Brad hated to admit that he had been using all of his might to keep from breaking down. Before Audra suggested dinner, Brad guided his mind away from the inevitable good-byes.

The Katy getaway had started as a plan to distance himself from people. But it had proved just the opposite. Days from now, memories of these people would surely keep playing in his mind. The woman who led them as guide. . .and as friend. Her right-hand man, a rock wall who said so much with so few words. The Pakistani entrepreneur who showed devotion to his altruistic wife. The fire-headed college guy who taught Brad to laugh at irritations and to let down his guard enough to make the ordinary into a comedy routine.

At least Brad would keep adding to his memories with the sixth rider. In his opinion, she was the most beautiful, warm-hearted one of the bunch. And his most devoted admirer.

Brad smiled at the sight of Hank. The redhead had pressed his cheek against the window, his warm breath steaming up the glass. The patch of steam grew and receded in rhythm with the young man's faint snores.

Sonya rested her head on Brad's shoulder. Amazing how strong he saw her now. Once a whiny dependent, she was now a woman who had biked across Missouri. But more than that, she was the one who detected the slightest pain in Judy's eyes and swept in without hesitation to hold her up. She'd proven her physical strength in an indisputable way—her inner strength in the form of God-given love.

Before long, Fletcher put the van into park and pulled out the key. "Harry's Diner!" he boomed, loud enough to startle Hank into knocking his head against the moist glass.

The greasy-spoon diner revisited the fifties, and their waitress fit the theme. Teenaged, perhaps, with a bandana and a stained apron. She chewed on the end of her pen as Brad placed his requests. "A pork chop sandwich with a side of onion rings."

Sonya, on the other hand, was easing back into her previous patterns—the ones she'd established since she started training. "Will you split the shake with me, Brad? And can I have a couple of your onion rings?"

After each hungry biker put in his order, Judy asked, "What are you all doing when you get home? Anything unusual?"

"Back to class," Hank said.

"Work," Audra answered, pointing to Amir. "And kids," she added, aiming a finger at herself.

Sonya knew Brad's answer, but he explained, too. To be sociable. "I'm back at Area Gym. . .and Sonya's visiting soon. Isn't that right, honey?"

"Not soon enough," she said, giving him a wink.

The food arrived in waxed paper and folded cardboard containers decorated with red crisscross patterns. Sonya nabbed her share of onion rings. Brad bit into his sandwich. He had to admit that, to him, the juicy chop could be featured in a four-star restaurant.

Audra wiped her mouth. "Amir and I are thinking of seeing what a Christian church is like when we get back to Kansas. There are dozens to choose from: little old buildings nestled in neighborhoods to some the size of Manhattan. Being in nature forces you to think about God, but being with people who know Him speaks even more loudly. You are such lovely people, so transparent. And through that transparency, Amir and I could see something we lacked. We can be so self-sufficient that it takes a million things to get our attention."

"Or not. Just a few timely words made the difference to me." Brad could swear Amir looked straight at him as he spoke. "I love my children. But as much as Audra and I give to them, we cannot provide everything they need. Our bank balance dips considerably after we pay for all the lessons and special activities we give our children. But their spirits need more than cultural enrichment. They need spiritual enrichment. And they need to see that in their parents above anyone else.

"Audra and I have not fully accepted your Christ. We are not impulsive people. If we make a decision, we will remain true to it. We want to know that we can, and want to, devote our lives to His calling."

Brad asked God to use him as His mouthpiece. "Well, if you do choose Christ—and I have a feeling that you will—He will use you to do great things with that kind of dedication."

Audra put down her burger. "I've always aspired to do great things, but I never thought about *God* using me to do His great things. I've looked to so many sources for direction, but I've always had a queasy feeling depending on my shrink for accountability. I love my friends, but they aren't tuned into their spiritual sides all that much either," Audra said. "Sometimes after I talk with them, I wish I'd never opened my mouth. The advice they give me comes straight from soap opera scripts, I'm afraid. Anyway, going to church will cost a lot less than therapy, that's for sure."

Brad was thinking it, but Sonya said it. "I wouldn't count on that, Audra."

"What do you mean?" she asked, not seeming alarmed, but interested.

Sonya said, "The greatest gifts have the greatest prices. It's not always easy to follow Christ. But if you stand firm, the rewards are deep. Like this trip. Sore muscles, sunburns, exhaustion. But even in the middle of the pain, we had a sense of satisfaction. And we'd all agree that getting here was worth every hardship."

Hank chirped up. "Are you saying that heaven is like Harry's Diner?" Brad knew him well enough to interpret the true meaning of his words. *I'm listening, too.*

"We sometimes forget, though," Brad said, looking at

Sonya. "We lose sight of the gifts God gives us. And we lose sight of Him."

Sonya smiled. "I'm glad He never loses sight of us."

"Yes, me, too."

❧

Brad's straw sputtered as he slurped the last of the pistachio shake. Striped paper baskets now held only spots of grease and smears of ketchup where fry cooks once stacked onion rings and burgers.

Audra looked at her watch. "We've still got another hour before the shuttle comes," she said. "I'm gonna call Mom. I bet she's up to her eyeballs in kids by now." Suddenly a thought popped into Brad's mind. He held it captive until Audra returned.

Brad leaned forward and whispered. "Where's the phone?"

"By the rest room," Audra whispered back, as if they shared a secret.

"Excuse me," he said louder and headed there.

Brad fished through his pockets and pulled out his calling card from his wallet. Looking at the back, he began to press a sequence of metal dial buttons.

"Hello?"

"Hi, Leslie," Brad said.

"Brad? That you? Did you survive the brutal perils of the Katy Trail?"

"Yep. And your sister went the distance. Two hundred miles."

"Sonya? Wow! She there?"

"I'll put her on in a minute," Brad said. "But I was wondering—before I do—can I talk to Maggie?"

"Sure. She's picking the batter off of her corn dog, but I think I can drag her away for a minute." Leslie's voice became muffled. "Maggie. It's your daddy."

Another muffled voice. A little one squealing, "Daddy!"

Brad's heart melted.

The phone rustled. "He'wo?"

"Hi, Magpie. What's up?"

"I miss you," the little voice said. "I want you back."

He thought, *You'll get me back. All of me. You'll get a dad who's present and wants to be, a dad who shows more love to you—and your mother.*

"I want you back, too," he said. "In fact, I was thinking that next week we could go to Kangaroo College, that place with all the crafts. I hear you can design your own kaleidoscope."

Phone line crackles filled Brad's ears.

"Would you like that? Maggie?"

"*You* want to go to Kangaroo College?" she asked.

"With you."

Brad's daughter's voice called away from the phone. "Guess what, Aunt Leslie! Daddy's gonna take me to Kangaroo College!"

"I'm also going to help you get ready more often and read you bedtime stories. Stuff like that."

"But Mommy's always done that stuff."

He'd expected that.

"Yes, but—"

"But maybe I can help you learn. I know how to read all my alphabet sounds and some blend together letters, too. So I can help you."

Brad smiled. "I'd like that."

"When are you coming home, Daddy?"

"That's one reason I called. Let me talk to Aunt Leslie about that."

"Okay. I love you."

"You can bet your corn dog that I love you, too, Magpie."

"Here's Aunt Leslie back."

Brad explained the happenings of the last few hours to his sister-in-law. And, in hushed tones he asked her a few questions. "Hope that's okay," he finally said.

"That will work fine."

"Leslie, you're an angel. Thanks." Brad pressed his hand over the mouthpiece and called over dish clinks and gossip murmurings. "Sonya! Come here!"

She didn't hear him, but he saw Audra tap her shoulder and point. Sonya waved in acknowledgement and slid out of the booth.

Once next to Brad, she gestured toward the phone. "Who's that?"

"Leslie. I wanted to talk to Maggie and square away last-minute details."

Sonya raised her eyebrows and shot an approving smile. "Okay." Holding out her hand, she asked, "May I?"

This could cost a day's salary. But with a smile, Brad handed his wife the phone.

thirty-two

"Hey, sis. I hear you showed that trail who's boss." Leslie's laugh vibrated the phone.

"Who told you that?" Sonya asked, looking at Brad through slitted eyes. He leaned against a doorframe, still smiling at her. Her eyes softened as she giggled. "I think I know already. Hey, Les, give Maggie my love. I would say hi, but I don't want to run up the bill. Plus, we'll be home tomorrow anyway."

Leslie laughed. "Yeah, right. . .tomorrow. See ya when you get here."

"What's so funny?"

"Eat that corn dog, kid. It's a wiener; you don't have to peel it," Leslie said, evidently not to Sonya. Then, "I better go. Maggie's starting to practice for Kangaroo College with her dinner."

Nothing Leslie was saying made a smidgen of sense.

"Bye, Les."

"See ya later, Sonya."

Click.

Sonya and Brad sank back in their booth.

"Hate to do this to you," Judy said, rising. "But we need to free up these tables for other hungry folks."

Brad stood, offered his hand, and pulled Sonya to her feet. They found their usual spots in the van for the last time.

Between a full stomach and muscles that finally decided to collapse, Sonya could hardly keep her eyes open. She found Brad's shoulder again, snuggled into his side, and drifted off before Fletcher could begin his next steering wheel solo.

After an unknown passage of time, Sonya heard Brad's soft voice. "We're here."

When Sonya opened her eyes, she saw the others filing out

of the van. Instead of sitting up, she readjusted herself, putting her arm around her husband's waist.

"We're back at the trailhead. The shuttle should be here any minute," Brad tried again. Sonya felt her husband's chest rumble as he laughed. "I can tell it's going to take that little extra to get you moving."

With that, he leaned over and kissed her.

Sonya sighed. "I can hardly stand the thought of moving this body again. And the thought of starting the drive home after the shuttle run is cruel torture. How long do we have to drive tonight?"

"That was the little extra I wanted to tell you about," Brad said.

"What little extra?"

"Well, I talked to Leslie, and she's all for it."

Sonya shook her head. "You're sounding like Hank that night at Lavina's House. Riddles and puzzles that don't make sense."

Brad continued. "Leslie said her schedule is not too bad for the next couple of days. Maggie's welcome to stay longer."

"What *are* you saying?"

"Here," Brad said. He opened her palm and pressed an object in it. A small, plastic lid with ridged sides. One that said, "YOU WON!"

A Letter To Our Readers

Dear Reader:

In order that we might better contribute to your reading enjoyment, we would appreciate your taking a few minutes to respond to the following questions. We welcome your comments and read each form and letter we receive. When completed, please return to the following:

Fiction Editor
Heartsong Presents
PO Box 719
Uhrichsville, Ohio 44683

1. Did you enjoy reading *The Flat Marriage Fix* by Karen Hayse?
   ❏ Very much! I would like to see more books by this author!
   ❏ Moderately. I would have enjoyed it more if

   _____

   _____

   _____

2. Are you a member of **Heartsong Presents**? ❏ Yes ❏ No
   If no, where did you purchase this book? _____

   _____

3. How would you rate, on a scale from 1 (poor) to 5 (superior), the cover design? _____

4. On a scale from 1 (poor) to 10 (superior), please rate the following elements.

   ____ Heroine   ____ Plot
   ____ Hero   ____ Inspirational theme
   ____ Setting   ____ Secondary characters

5. These characters were special because?_____
_____
_____

6. How has this book inspired your life?_____
_____
_____

7. What settings would you like to see covered in future **Heartsong Presents** books? _____
_____
_____

8. What are some inspirational themes you would like to see treated in future books? _____
_____
_____

9. Would you be interested in reading other **Heartsong Presents** titles? ❏ Yes ❏ No

10. Please check your age range:
   ❏ Under 18 ❏ 18-24
   ❏ 25-34 ❏ 35-45
   ❏ 46-55 ❏ Over 55

Name_____
Occupation _____
Address _____
City_____ State_____ Zip_____